"Andrea, I Had To Leave..."

"Really? And you couldn't have taken the time to say goodbye in person? You had to leave a message on my home phone at a time when you knew I'd be sitting at my desk at work? 'Andrea, I'm sorry, but I can't marry you. I'm leaving town and I won't be back. Forget about me,'" Andrea mimicked Clay's voice, hating the fact that hers cracked over the last phrase.

Clay swallowed. "It's the best I could do at the time."

"I don't want an apology, I want an explanation."

He held Andrea's gaze and shook his head. "An apology is all I'm offering."

"That's not good enough."

She tried to step around him, but he caught her upper arms, pushed her back a step and kicked the door closed.

Oh, hell. Like it or not, it looked like they were going to duke this out now.

Dear Reader,

Shopping for our family's tiny ski boat a decade ago is a far cry from buying a yacht and in no way prepared me to write this book. Lucky for me, there is a yacht-building facility similar to Dean Yachts a few hours from my home, and they offer free tours. Since I know zilch about yachts I enlisted the help of more knowledgeable sources—my brother and his friend, both yacht owners, and my oldest son, a male, and therefore fascinated with anything possessing a big engine.

The facility was nothing like I expected. Security and safety were prime concerns, but that's where my preconceived notions died. This wasn't a sterile factory. Instead, there truly was a family atmosphere amongst the employees. I can only hope I did the friendly and knowledgeable staff justice in my version. And while the characters in my book are all make-believe, famous race-car drivers have been known to buy their exquisite yachts here in North Carolina, and I can see why. These luxurious watercrafts are truly an inspiration.

Enjoy,

Emilie Rose

EMILIE ROSE

Exposing the Executive's Secrets

Published by Silhouette Books
America's Publisher of Contemporary Romance

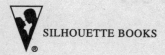

SILHOUETTE BOOKS
®

ISBN-13: 978-0-373-76738-0
ISBN-10:   0-373-76738-2

EXPOSING THE EXECUTIVE'S SECRETS

Books by Emilie Rose

Silhouette Desire

Expecting Brand's Baby #1463
The Cowboy's Baby Bargain #1511
The Cowboy's Million-Dollar Secret #1542
A Passionate Proposal #1578
Forbidden Passion #1624
Breathless Passion #1635
Scandalous Passion #1660
Condition of Marriage #1675
*Paying the Playboy's Price #1732
*Exposing the Executive's Secrets #1738

*Trust Fund Affairs

EMILIE ROSE

lives in North Carolina with her college-sweetheart husband and four sons. This bestselling author's love for romance novels developed when she was twelve years old and her mother hid them under sofa cushions each time Emilie entered the room. Emilie grew up riding and showing horses. She's a devoted baseball mom during the season and can usually be found in the bleachers watching one of her sons play. Her hobbies include quilting, cooking (especially cheesecake) and anything cowboy. Her favorite TV shows include Discovery Channel's medical programs, *ER, CSI* and *Boston Public*. Emilie's a country music fan because there's an entire book in nearly every song.

Emilie loves to hear from her readers and can be reached at P.O. Box 20145, Raleigh, NC 27619 or at www.EmilieRose.com.

Kira,

Your words are magical.
Thanks for putting me in the gondola.

One

"This one's going to come back to bite you, Andrea. Please choose another bachelor."

Andrea Montgomery's heart bumped along faster than a roller coaster. Her stomach alternated between the rise of anticipation and the plunge of trepidation. She sipped her complimentary champagne, tucked her numbered bidding paddle beneath her arm and then reached for her dearest friend's hand and squeezed.

"Holly, I can't. You know I have to do this."

"Buying him is a mistake. Remember how torn up you were when he left?"

As if I could forget that kind of pain.

"That was then. I'm *totally* over him now." And she was. Absolutely. Without a doubt. How could she not be over a man who'd led her on for years and then dumped her without giving her a believable reason?

Andrea released Holly's fingers and then plucked at the black silk charmeuse of her gown. What little fabric there was in the garment clung to her like a second skin. The neckline plunged almost to her navel, and if the slit in the ankle-length skirt were an inch higher no one would have to wonder whether or not she wore panties.

She shifted on her stiletto heels—the only part of the outfit she liked—and scanned the crowd of overexcited, expensively attired women consuming free champagne and bidding on bachelors. No one in this affluent, conservative country club crowd suffered from the same overexposure as her.

"What were you and Juliana thinking when you chose this dress? As much as I love sexy clothing, this gown is too obvious and over the top. Couldn't you have chosen something more subtle? Subtle is sexy. Obvious is tacky. I feel like a high-priced call girl. No wait. Even a working girl would leave a little mystery and cover more skin."

Holly didn't even crack a smile. "When seduction's the name of the game you bring out the big guns. You're planning to bring Clayton Dean to his knees. Juliana and I thought you should dress the part of femme fatale."

Clayton Dean. Hearing his name wound Andrea's nerves tighter. "You've miscast me. A femme fatale seduces the man in question. I have no intention of revisiting the sheets with Clay. He had his chance eight years ago and blew it. And how many times do I have to tell you? I'm not out for revenge. All I want to do is show him that there are no hard feelings."

"Uh-huh." Holly didn't attempt to hide her skepticism.

Her friend knew her too well. "Okay, so I won't mind if he eats his heart out just a little over what he could have had. But that's all. I'd be a fool to hand him my heart again."

"I agree. That's why I'm going to keep repeating, *this is a bad idea* like a broken record until you get it."

"Holly, I've lived through the humiliation of Clay dumping me once. My coworkers' pity was hard enough to swallow the first time. And according to Mrs. Dean, Clay's staying in Wilmington only until his father is well enough to return to the helm at Dean Yachts, and then Clay will sail back to Florida. I promise I won't forget this is temporary."

"You're trying awfully hard to sell yourself on a bad idea, Ms. Marketing Director."

"Cut it out. Remember this is not just about me. Without Clay the business might have to temporarily shut its doors, putting me and a thousand other employees out of work. Joseph Dean has been like a second father to me. I've been worried about his mood since his stroke three weeks ago. He and Clay need to work this out before it's too late." The possibility of losing her mentor put a lump in her throat.

Holly's frown deepened. "What if father and son do kiss and make up and Clay returns for good? He'll be your boss. Will you still love your job then?"

Andrea winced. Good point. Darn it. As if she didn't have a boatload of doubts already about working with Clay. "I need to move forward. I can't do that until I put the past behind me. I'm a loser magnet, Holly. I have to break the cycle, and to do that I need to know what's so wrong with me that Clay and every guy I've dated in the past eight years dumps me just when I start to believe there might be something to the relationship."

Holly stamped her foot in irritation. "I could smack you. How many times do I have to tell you there's nothing wrong with you?"

"Says you."

Holly's attention shifted to something beyond Andrea's shoulder. "I hope you're right about being over him, because Clay looks good. Really, really good."

Andrea choked on her champagne. After catching her breath she discarded the flute on a passing waiter's tray and braced herself before following Holly's gaze to the other side of the opulent Caliber Club ballroom. Her first glimpse of her former lover knocked the wind right back out of her.

Clay did look good. Amazing, in fact. Damn him. The last thing she wanted or needed was to still find him attractive. His shoulders were broader than she remembered, and his tuxedo hinted at muscles he hadn't possessed as a lanky twenty-three-year-old. A nostalgic smile tugged her lips. He may look more sophisticated, but he still hadn't learned to tame his beaver-brown hair. The longer strands on top curled in disarray just as they had after she'd rumpled them when they made lo—

She severed the thought instantly. No need to travel that heavily rutted dead end road again.

She didn't think he'd spotted her yet, and she wanted to keep it that way—right up until she bought him. A combination of anticipation and unease traversed her spine.

"Putting the past to bed will be worth every penny I have to bid on bachelor number thirteen tonight."

One of Holly's eyebrows lifted. "Bed? Freudian slip?"

Andrea scowled at her friend. "You know what I mean. I want this over and done with. Final. Finished. Forgotten."

"If you say so." The doubt in Holly's voice didn't instill confidence. "We knew our trust funds would come in handy one day, but I don't think our granddaddies intended us to buy men—even if it is for a charitable cause. Juliana certainly dropped a bundle on her rebel."

Juliana had been the first in their close-knit trio to buy her man. Andrea hoped her straight-laced friend could handle the rebellious biker bar owner. "I hope that goes well."

"Amen. I hope none of us regret tonight's nonsense."

"Holly, we agreed—"

"No, you and Juliana agreed. My arm was twisted, but I'm in for better or worse."

The gavel sounded like a starter's pistol. Andrea nearly jumped out of her skimpy dress. Bachelor twelve left the stage to meet his date, and the women in the audience went wild in anticipation of the next offering. She covered her ears as the decibel level rose and wondered if she should chalk this foolish plan up to too many margaritas and walk away.

No. She couldn't. She wanted a life and that meant dealing with her messy, painful past. The band's drum roll rattled in tandem with her rapidly thumping pulse as the emcee announced the next bachelor.

Her bachelor. Clayton Dean.

Andrea pushed the tousled mass of her hair—the style another contribution from her friends—away from her face. Sure, she talked a good game by pretending that buying and confronting the man who'd shattered her heart and her confidence eight years ago was going to be a piece of cake, but her insides quivered and her knees knocked beneath her trampy dress. She'd loved Clay, had planned to marry him, have his children and run Dean Yachts by his side. His abrupt departure had nearly destroyed her.

What if her plan went terribly wrong?

She squared her shoulders and squashed her doubts. It wouldn't. At thirty years old she was more than mature enough to face a former lover without making a fool of herself. Besides, she'd strategized every last detail—the same way she would an extensive marketing campaign.

Buy him, thereby obligating him to seven dates and giving her seven opportunities to:

Impress him with her acquired business savvy.

Tempt him, but keep her distance.

Question him to find out why she was so easy to leave.

Dismiss him from her heart and her head.

The women surrounding her screamed maniacally as Clay took his place center stage. Who wouldn't want a series of dates with a handsome naval architect and award-winning yacht designer? But she was determined that Clay would be hers. *Temporarily.* Andrea clenched her numbered fan so tightly the wooden handle cracked.

An omen? Goose bumps raced over her skin.

Holly leaned closer and spoke directly into Andrea's ear to be heard above the din. "Are you sure you can handle Seven Seductive Sunsets with Clay?"

"Of course." She waved away Holly's concern, but tucked her free hand behind her back when she realized her fingers trembled.

And then she lifted her paddle and cast the first bid on her former lover—the man who would soon be her boss.

If he didn't love her, he'd kill her. Clay glared at his mother as he took the stage.

Smile, she mouthed and pointed to her own curving lips.

He turned a big, phony smile to the crowd. His mother could have warned him about the bachelor auction for charity, but no, she'd planned the date package, put his picture in the auction program and then shanghaied him the moment he'd docked today. He'd tried to buy his way out of this fiasco with a hefty donation, but nobody bulldozed Patricia Dean once she set her mind to something, and she'd set her mind toward making a fool of her only son.

But he owed her, so he let her get away with it.

As if he didn't have enough on his plate running his own company, he had to take control of Dean Yachts until he could hire an interim CEO. That meant working with Andrea, Dean's marketing manager, on a daily basis. Regret tightened like a fist around his heart.

He did not want to be here—not back in his hometown or up on this stage being auctioned off like a repossessed yacht. There was too much flotsam under the bridge, and there were too many disappointments, too many broken promises.

The women—tipsy from the sounds of it—called out lewd suggestions, but he'd be damned if he'd shake his wares or prance around like a male striper for his audience. If the other bachelors wanted to act like fools fine, but he wouldn't. Being stuck babysitting some bubble-headed socialite was already beyond the call of duty.

Clay stood in the hot lights as stiff as a mast. One spotlight baked his skin. Another panned the crowd as the emcee rattled off Clay's vital statistics. Staring out at the hysterical women, he mentally dared any one of them to buy him.

And then he saw her—*Andrea*—in the crowd. His lungs deflated like a sail without a breeze and his stomach shriveled into a hot lump of coal. Damn. What was she doing here? He'd thought he had until Monday to prepare himself for seeing her again.

He'd loved her—almost enough to turn a blind eye to the discovery that had knocked his foundations out from under him.

The spotlight shifted back to the stage, blinding him. The bid climbed higher, *embarrassingly high* compared to the last two saps. He should be proud he wasn't going as low as a junked schooner, but he wasn't. He wanted off the stage. The sooner, the better. The bidders used numbered paddles instead of calling out bids, and he couldn't see who wielded the numbers because of the damned lights, so he didn't have a clue who bid what.

The gavel hit the podium. "Sold," the emcee shouted. "Come and collect your prize, number two-twenty-one."

Good. Finally over—at least the first part of his torture. Clay gladly vacated the stage. His eyes adjusted to the dimness at the bottom of the stairs in time to see Andrea hand a check to the woman behind the desk. Shock locked his muscles.

Andrea had bought him!

He caught a glimpse of her wavy blond hair and cara-mel-colored eyes a split second before the visual impact of her black dress nearly knocked him to his knees. Her pale breasts poised on the brink of spilling from the gashing deep neckline, and a slit cut nearly to her crotch displayed one long, satiny leg. His breath lodged in his throat and he almost swallowed his tongue. Heat exploded in his groin.

Mayday. Mayday.

She strolled in his direction, smiling at him with a cool confidence he didn't recall her having when she'd been his lover. "Hello, Clay. Shall we find a quiet corner and make our arrangements?"

Her voice slid through him like smooth, aged whiskey. How could he have forgotten her soft, southern drawl or the temperature-raising effect it had on him?

"Hold it," a thirtyish African American woman called out. A tall, pale guy holding a camera stood beside her. The woman made a squeezing motion with her hands. Clay moved closer to Andrea. "Arms around each other, please, and smile."

Clay gritted his teeth into a smile and put his arm around Andrea. His palm found bare skin. Damnation. The back of her dress was as bare as the front. Her body heat seared his palm and penetrated his tux jacket. Fire streaked through him. Fire he had to extinguish. Right now.

Andrea gasped, nearly expelling her breasts from the shiny black fabric. Clay couldn't help himself. His gaze shifted to her creamy skin. And the camera flashed. Oh hell. Caught looking. Before he could ask the reporter to take another shot Andrea pulled free, pivoted on her very sexy heels and strolled away with a mind-altering sway to her hips.

Whoa. That was not the same woman he'd left behind. The Andrea he'd known would never have worn a dress guaranteed to make a man forget his manners and his name.

Reeling from the unwelcome slam of desire, he shook his head and caught sight of his mother's smug smile. She was up to something—something he was certain would make him regret coming home more than he already did.

Clay followed Andrea toward the door. After the way he'd left her he'd expected her to want him dead.

Why would she come to his rescue tonight?

And what would it cost him?

"What game are you playing, Andrea?" Clay's voice rumbled over her, deep and familiar, but with a rough edge Andrea didn't remember.

Her heart raced and her breath came in short bursts—not caused solely by her hasty retreat from the prying eyes inside. She reached the deserted gazebo at the end of the dock jutting into the Cape Fear River and wished she could keep on walking. Despite two weeks of planning, she wasn't ready for this confrontation, but she braced herself and turned.

With the lights of the Caliber Club behind him, shadow concealed most of Clay's face. His cheeks appeared leaner and his jaw more sharply defined than eight years ago. Jagged streaks of moonlight reflected off the water in wavering beams. One slashed across his eyes making them a more intense blue than she recalled.

"I don't have time for games, Clay."

"Then what's this about?" He jerked a thumb, indicating the club. "A trip down memory lane?"

"Can't a woman rescue an old friend from the money-hungry masses without complaint?"

"Old friends. Is that what we are?"

Could they ever be friends again? Doubtful. But she could fake it long enough to get the closure she needed. "I hope so."

"So this is you being self-sacrificing?"

His sarcasm stiffened her spine and heated her cheeks with a not-so-subtle reminder that she'd been something of a pampered princess when he left town. But that had changed. She'd learned the hard way not to take anything for granted—like happiness, promises or loved ones. "You have a problem with that?"

"You never could lie worth a damn. You get a quiver in your voice. C'mon. Spill it, Andrea. Why are we really here?"

She cursed the telling sign of her agitation and cleared her throat. "We have to work together. So anything that makes your life easier makes my life easier. Saving you from that—" she gestured toward the club "—seemed like a nice thing to do."

"You're claiming this is about work?" More sarcasm. He clearly didn't buy her story. She couldn't blame him.

Pursing her lips, she exhaled in resignation. This wasn't going as well as she'd anticipated. She'd expected him to be grateful, not suspicious. "I need to know that I can count on you not to bail before Joseph's back on his feet."

His breath hissed. "I have my own business to run. I'll stay until the headhunting firm I've hired locates an interim CEO, and then I'm out of here."

She gaped and then snapped her mouth closed. "You can't hand Dean Yachts over to a stranger. Your father would—"

"My father has nothing so say about it," he interrupted in a flat don't-argue-with-me tone.

Reeling, she scrambled to make him understand. "The doctors expect Joseph to make an eighty to ninety percent recovery from the stroke. His mental faculties are clear, but his stamina isn't what it used to be. Knowing you'd be here is the only reason he agreed to stay out of the office while he recuperates."

A balmy June breeze whipped her hair across her face and ruffled the edges of her gown, nearly baring her breasts. Clay's gaze lowered to her cleavage. Her nipples peaked and an ache started deep inside her. Damn. It.

"I didn't ask for an update." Clay shifted deeper into the shadows. In the darkness she couldn't read his expression. Did he like what he saw? Did he have even one moment's regret for walking away from what they'd had? Had he thought about her at all since he'd left?

Stop it. It doesn't matter.

But it did. Andrea clenched her fingers around the long chain strap of her sequined evening bag.

"You should have. He's your father. In a couple of months he'll be back on the job unless you rush him and he ends up endangering his health. Give him time to heal, Clay."

He shoved his hands into his pockets and turned away, presenting her with his back—a broad, unyielding wall of resistance.

The creaking of the dock boards and the clang of the sailboat lines in the slips broke the silence, but the familiar sounds didn't have their usual calming effect.

Ask him why he left.

But she couldn't. Not yet. Because she wasn't sure she was ready to hear his answer. What if he told her something hideous and then she had to face him daily for the next few months? But she would get the information out of him before he left.

Andrea sighed and plucked a strand of hair from her overly glossy—thanks to her friends—lips. She joined Clay at the rail, and the citrus and spice scent of his cologne wafted to her on the breeze. Memories washed over her, tugging at her like a strong riptide. Memories of a night very like this one. High school graduation night. The tiny cabin of his sailboat. Making love for the first time. Learning his body as he learned hers.

Stop.

She shifted restlessly and pushed away the past. Okay, so she still found Clay physically appealing. Big deal. That didn't mean she'd let the current of attraction pull her under. He'd hurt her too badly for her to ever trust him again.

Stick to the agenda, Andrea. Focus on what you're good at—your job. And the rest will follow.

She took a deep breath and launched into her practiced spiel. "Dean Yachts has a backlog of pending orders. You'll have to plunge into the deep end if we're to keep up with our production schedule. Your father will tell you whatever you need to know to stay afloat."

His jaw hardened. "I don't need his help."

She bit her lip and battled frustration. Mending the breach between the men might be harder than she'd anticipated. "You may not need it, but Joseph needs you to ask for it. He's depressed and more than a little shaken up by his brush with mortality. He's looking forward to having you at home."

He turned his head and met her gaze. She'd never considered Clay inflexible or implacable in the past, but his face wore both traits now. His square jaw jutted forward. "I docked my boat at Dean's. I'm berthing there."

"Security didn't notify me."

"Mom cleared it before I arrived."

Neither Mrs. Dean nor security had informed Andrea, which was odd since Andrea was unofficially in charge at the moment. But then Mrs. Dean had been acting strangely since she'd let it slip that Clay would be coming home and arriving just in time to participate in the auction. But Andrea would worry about that later.

"You will go by the house to see your father, won't you?"

"No."

Another wave of frustration crashed over Andrea's head. "Clay, Joseph needs his family around him."

"It's a little late for him to start thinking about his family." Bitterness tightened his voice.

"What does that mean?" He remained silent and Andrea's irritation and curiosity mounted. What had happened eight years ago to cause this rift? "It's never too late to say you're sorry."

He pivoted sharply. Moonlight illuminated the flattened line of his mouth and his narrowed eyes. "Is that what you want? An apology?"

She gasped. As if an apology would be enough to fix what he'd done. "I wasn't talking about me. I meant you and Joseph. He's your father, Clay. *Wake up.* You could have lost him. Take this opportunity to fix things between you before it's too late. You might not get another chance."

"You don't know what you're talking about."

"Then explain it to me." She crushed her evening bag in her fingers, half hoping, half fearing his answer.

He made a scoffing sound. "You couldn't handle it."

"Try me." A minute dragged past. Two.

"It's over, Andrea. Let it go."

If only she could, but even now Clay's nearness stirred

things best left undisturbed. She traveled a few shaky steps down the dock being careful to keep her heels from getting caught between the boards. "Just in case you're worried, I'm not interested in picking up where we left off. But we have to work together, Clay. I need your support in front of the staff."

"You'll have it." He shadowed her down the dock. "Mother says you've single-handedly run the company for the past three weeks."

Was that grudging respect in his voice? "I've done what I could, but we have over a thousand employees. It's been a true team effort."

"Why can't you continue without me?"

"Because people expect a Dean to be at the helm of Dean Yachts, and we need someone capable of coordinating all the teams involved in production. I can't do that." She paused and turned. "About these dates…I'm not expecting, nor do I want, the romance promised in your auction package."

"My mother's auction package," he corrected. "I had nothing to do with it. She planned the entire thing. I'm just her damned puppet."

Why didn't that surprise her? "Whatever. I want us to be civil, to show folks that there are no hard feelings. Reputation is everything in yacht building, and I don't want any rumors of dissention inside the company spreading or Dean's will lose business. If you have any problems with me or my work, then I'd prefer you keep them to yourself until we're away from prying eyes."

He swore. A muscle in his jaw twitched. "I'm sorry if I hurt you. If we could go back—"

If he'd hurt her? She choked a humorless laugh at the absurdity of his comment and held up a hand, halting his words. "Would you still leave?"

He raked his fingers through his hair, stared across the water. Ten seconds ticked past and then he exhaled. "Yes."

Somehow she managed not to stagger under the impact of his reply. Clay couldn't possibly know how badly he'd hurt and humiliated her eight years ago. She would never give him—or any other man for that matter—the power to do so again. Never.

"That's all I need to know. I'll see you Monday, Clay."

Two

Traversing the wide sidewalk leading from the docks to Dean Yachts on Monday morning felt like coming home. But home was somewhere Clay no longer belonged.

Perched high on a grassy knoll overlooking the Cape Fear River, the sales and marketing division looked more like an expensive beach house than the main offices of Dean Yachts. When he reached the front doors Clay turned. From this vantage point he could see the entire operation.

A series of pale blue metal buildings in a range of shapes and sizes spread along a half-mile section of the riverfront property. Each building housed a specific stage of production, and Clay had worked in every one of them in one capacity or another beginning in his early teens. Both his grandfather and his father believed in learning the business from the ground up.

During Clay's absence murals of various Dean Yachts'

models had been painted on the waterfront sides of the structures giving the impression of a life-size parade of boats heading into port.

Docks, some covered, some not, jutted from the shoreline. The slips held yachts nearing completion. Unless things had changed in eight years, the dock located directly behind the sales office was reserved for finished vessels awaiting delivery. His and one other occupied the slips.

Clay let his gaze run over the complex again and sadness weighted him like ballast. He'd once taken pride in knowing that one day all this would be his. But not anymore. He'd forfeited everything when he'd run from the truth.

Shaking off the bitter memory and the resulting sense of anger, betrayal and disappointment, he shoved open the wide glass door, stepped inside the reception area and jerked to a halt. Nothing looked the same. What once had been a dim, utilitarian entrance now looked as classy as the stateroom of a fine yacht. Sunlight streamed through the windows and skylights onto a gleaming teak floor. A gracefully curved reception counter had replaced the old metal desk, and beyond that a glass wall blocked the wide hall leading to the offices.

The young woman seated behind the desk looked up and flashed him a smile that could sell toothpaste. "Good morning, sir. May I help you?"

"I'm Clayton Dean."

Her smile dimmed a few watts and she sat up straighter. "One moment please. I'll let Ms. Montgomery know you're here. You're welcome to have a seat while you wait."

A flip of her hand indicated the leather seating group against the wall. Another change. "No need. I'll find her."

The woman sprang from her chair and blocked his path. "I'm sorry, Mr. Dean, you'll have to wait until Ms. Montgomery gives you clearance."

What? "Clearance?"

"You'll need a security pass." She punched a button on the gadget clipped to her belt and spoke quietly into her nearly invisible headset receiver. "Mr. Dean has arrived."

Had he stepped into the *Twilight Zone?* When he'd left eight years ago Dean's hadn't had any security other than locking the buildings at night and occasional drive-by from the sheriff's department. This morning the back door closest to the dock—the entrance Clay had used since he was a kid—had been locked, and yesterday he'd had a sticky encounter with several members of the security crew when he'd taken his motorcycle out for supplies and to arrange for delivery of a rental car. They'd called his mother before letting him pass back through the gate.

"She'll be right with you, Mr. Dean." The receptionist punctuated her words with another high-wattage smile.

Clay couldn't sit. This building held too many memories. Good ones. Bad ones. A flicker of movement drew his attention to the glass wall. Andrea strode down the hall. Her figure-skimming sage-green suit was as professional as Saturday night's black dress had been drop-dead sexy. She'd twisted her thick blond hair up onto her head revealing the long, pale line of her throat. The polished woman before him was the antithesis of the unsure girl he'd left behind.

A section of the glass glided open. "Thanks, Eve. I'll take it from here. Good morning, Clay. Please come with me."

Andrea's gaze briefly hit his and then she headed back the way she'd come before he had a chance to reply. His gaze automatically shifted to the curve of her hips as he followed her down the hall. She'd always had a killer walk. Her perfume tantalized him. It wasn't the sweet flowery scent he remembered. This fragrance had a spicy and alluring kick to it.

He cursed his response. Rekindling the old flame was out of the question. He could not stay in Wilmington and face the lie that continued to erode his pilings on a daily basis.

Had his father kept his word? Clay couldn't ask and doubted he'd get an honest answer if he did. How could he trust anything his father said anymore? How could he trust himself with that DNA?

His muscles dragged like metal against rust-covered metal as they approached his father's office. Struggling to get a handle on the emotions welling inside him, Clay paused in the corridor. He clenched and unclenched his hands as memories assailed him.

The last time he'd taken this walk he'd been on top of the world. He'd come home from the University of New Orleans a day early to ask his father to go with him to buy Andrea's engagement ring, and then he'd opened the door without knocking and his world had crashed.

Determined to face yet another specter from his past Clay forced himself forward. Every stick of the old office furniture—including the damned couch where Clay had found his father screwing Andrea's mother—had been replaced with expensive-looking classic pieces.

He caught Andrea's guarded gaze and noted her pinched expression. Did she know what had happened right here under her nose? She and her mother had always had an enviably close relationship, the kind of link he'd never shared with his father. If Andrea didn't know about the affair, she'd be just as disillusioned by her mother's behavior as he had been by his father's. He wouldn't do that to her.

He jerked his head toward the door. "What's with all the new security?"

"We're protecting our assets. Our base-price yachts cost

a million dollars. Most of the models we build far exceed that. We can't risk vandalism or theft." She gestured for him to take a seat behind the cherry desk and tapped on a sheaf of papers waiting on the blotter with a pale pink—not red like Saturday night—fingernail. "I need you to read and sign these."

He remained standing, but lifted the pages and read a few paragraphs. Surprise forced his head up. "What is this?"

"A noncompete clause. Nothing you see or learn here can be used to compete against Dean designs."

"You're joking."

"No, I'm not. You're a naval architect with your own design firm, but temporarily you're an employee here. We have to take precautions against our ideas being pirated."

Fury boiled in his veins at the insult to his ethics. He fought to contain it. "You expect me to run the place, but this," he rattled the sheets, "says you don't trust me."

Her lips firmed and her chin lifted. "It's a business decision, Clay. Emotion doesn't enter into it."

Bitterness filled his mouth. *He* wasn't the cheat in his family. "My father's idea?"

A defiant glint entered her eyes and a flush rose in her pale cheeks. "No. Mine."

That doused his anger like nothing else could. He had no right to complain. He'd earned Andrea's distrust. He skimmed the pages, scratched his name across the line at the bottom of the page and passed the document to her.

She nodded acceptance. "I've left the current order summary and a packet of info to reacquaint you with the company in your in-box. You'll need to familiarize yourself with our existing client roster since they're allowed to drop in at anytime to check the status of their project. I'd suggest you look through those documents until Fran, your administrative assistant arrives. She comes in at nine. Her office is through here." She shoved open a door on the starboard side of the room.

Andrea acted like a car show model—gesturing stiffly here and there, making minimal eye contact, but he noticed the slight tremor of the pages she held. Another needle of regret stabbed him. He and Andrea had once been as comfortable together as two lovers could be.

"When Fran arrives she'll make your security ID and fit you with the necessary safety equipment. You'll need to swipe the ID card to access the controlled areas and the front gate. We have one delivery tomorrow and another next week. Both are noted on your calendar. There's quite a bit of hoopla attached to delivery celebrations. Again, Fran will fill you in.

"I've scheduled a production walk-through at three this afternoon for you. My office is still where it used to be if you need anything." She headed for the door.

"Andrea." He waited until she turned. "I won't work in here. My office is out there." He pointed toward the wide window overlooking the water. *The Expatriate,* one of his own designs, rocked beside the dock to the rear of the sales office.

Her eyebrows dipped. "You expect me to trot out to the dock every time I need to speak to you?"

"Either that or call my cell phone." He extracted a business card from his wallet and wrote his cell number on it. He passed it to her and their fingers brushed. The contact hit him like a bolt of lightning.

Strictly business, Dean.

"I'll see if I can have maintenance run a phone line to your boat."

"You said my assistant's name is Fran. Your mother changed positions?"

"No. Mom doesn't work here anymore. She left years ago."

Good. One less ghost he'd have to face.

Day One. Six hours successfully behind her, and three more, including Clay's tour, to get through before Andrea could call it a day.

As she made her way down the dock to Clay's "office" after lunch she ran an assessing gaze over the sleek lines of the fifty-foot sport-fishing vessel. Nice. Habit and just plain good manners forced her to remove her heels before ascending the ramp to Clay's boat rather than risk damaging his deck.

Andrea usually reserved her finer suits for delivery celebrations. When a customer accepted ownership of their new yacht the Dean's sales staff wined and dined them with a champagne feast. There wasn't an event today, but she'd had an attack of vanity this morning knowing this was Clay's first day on the job.

Before she entered the production buildings later this afternoon to reintroduce Clay to the area managers she'd have to dig her rubber-soled deck shoes out from under her desk. It wouldn't be the first time she'd worn a designer suit with her Docksides. If she'd been less vain she'd be wearing the boat shoes now instead of carrying her heels.

She spotted Clay through the glass-topped door leading to the salon. His laptop sat open and ignored on one end of the galley table he'd turned into a desk while he flipped through a stack of familiar brochures—brochures she'd designed.

A combination of anxiety and pride eddied through her.

Dean Yachts had come a long way since he'd left, and Andrea was proud to have been instrumental in the change. Old school practices still reigned over modern technology in the production department, but that was because hand-crafted workmanship was part of Dean's appeal. No mass production here. But Joseph had allowed her to update the way they interacted with the public. She'd poured her heart into the Web page, the reception area, the offices and the brochures in Clay's hands.

She tapped on the glass and Clay looked up. His cobalt-blue gaze locked with hers, momentarily impeding her ability to breathe. *Damn. It. Control yourself.*

He rose and crossed the room. Ignoring the stretch of his white short-sleeved polo shirt over his wide shoulders and muscular chest should have been easy, considering what he'd put her through, but it wasn't. Nor could she overlook the way his pants fit his lean hips and long legs. It wasn't fair that she still found him attractive after all the time and heartache she'd wasted on him. But she'd get over it.

The door opened, jarring her back to the present with a waft of cool air-conditioned air. Until then she'd been too antsy to notice the cloying June heat and humidity. Both were a fact of life on the Wilmington waterfront.

She cleared her throat. "May I come in? We need to discuss the image we intend to convey to the reporter. I realize this is work time and we shouldn't discuss personal issues, but I have plans for this evening."

Plans that included a pint of death by chocolate ice cream and a strategy phone call to Juliana and Holly, her partners in the auction scheme. She also needed to make sure Holly—who'd been reluctant about the whole bachelor auction idea—had bought the firefighter Andrea and Juliana had chosen from the program for her.

She didn't know how Clay did it, but without moving a muscle he seemed more alert, more wary. "What reporter?"

"Didn't you know the local paper is chronicling each auction couple for the duration of the dating package?"

He shoved a hand through his already disheveled hair and moved away from the door. She stepped through and closed it behind her.

"No. My mother shanghaied me as soon as I docked. I spent Saturday afternoon being fitted for a tux and arrived at the club minutes before I hit the stage—too late to read the hype and the fine print. Mom didn't tell me about the reporter or even what my date package involves. All I know about it is what I could hear of the emcee's spiel to the crowd."

Glancing around the cabin, Andrea took in the smoky gray leather seating and the rich cherry wood. Nice. Elegant, but masculine. She gestured to his laptop computer. "Do you have Internet access?"

"Yes. Wireless."

"May I?" At his nod she typed in a Web address. A few clicks later she read aloud, "The lucky lady who wins bachelor thirteen will be treated to Seven Seductive Sunsets, including an old-fashioned carriage ride through the historic section of town, horseback riding on a local beach, a riverboat dinner cruise, a hot air balloon ride, dinner and dancing at Devil's Shoals Steakhouse, a daylong sailing adventure and a private bonfire on the beach."

Was Clay swearing under his breath? She couldn't be certain because he turned and marched into the galley. A second later he returned and shoved a bottle of water in her direction.

"Are you willing to skip the dates? I'll reimburse you what you paid for the package."

"Try explaining that to the reporter. Bad press."

His jaw muscles flexed. "There's no way out of this?"

"Dating me didn't used to be a hardship." Andrea mentally kicked herself. Nothing like showing your damaged ego.

"No. It wasn't."

Her gaze bounced back to Clay's and her heart missed a beat at the intensity in his eyes. *Don't do it. Don't get sucked under. Tempt him, but keep your distance.* She dampened her lips and belatedly accepted the water from him. The chilled bottle helped her regain her focus.

"But that was then. Now we're two professionals who stand to gain quite a bit of publicity for our respective businesses if we conduct ourselves appropriately."

His lips thinned. "That's what this is to you? A publicity stunt?"

"That and an opportunity for us to put the past behind us and move on." She gestured to the salon and galley. "This looks quite…homey."

He leaned his hip against the galley counter and crossed his ankles, drawing her attention to his leather deck shoes worn without socks, and the sprinkling of dark hair peeking out from beneath the hem of his pants. "That's because it is home."

"For now, you mean."

He shook his head. "I live on *The Expatriate*."

"Permanently?" She couldn't conceal her surprise.

"Yes."

She curled her bare toes into the lush cream-colored carpeting and shifted her weight from one foot to the other as she scanned the interior again looking for signs of a feminine occupant. "Will we need a gate pass for anyone else on board?"

"I live alone."

Relief rushed over her—relief she had no business feeling. "Have you ever owned a home? Besides a boat, I mean."

They'd once talked of buying a house on the beach with a long expanse of sand on which their dogs and children could run. She'd bought the house, but lacked the children and pets. Having recently turned thirty she'd decided that if she wanted those factors to change—and she did—then she had to get the ball rolling.

His jaw hardened. "I had an apartment over a marina when I first moved to Miami. After I designed and commissioned my first yacht I moved on board. I've been living on the water ever since."

"That certainly makes it easy to move." She bit her imprudent tongue when his eyes hardened.

"Easy to leave, you mean?"

Be nice. Do not pick a fight. "That's not what I said."

"You want to take off the gloves?"

"I beg your pardon?"

His gaze drifted from the V-neck of her pantsuit to her bare feet and back to her eyes. Sensation rippled in the wake of his thorough inspection and ended up tangling in a knot behind her naval. "You're clenching your fingers and even your toes. Are you spoiling for a fight, Andrea?"

"Of course not," she answered quickly—too quickly, judging by his raised eyebrow. She hated that he could read her so easily. Exhaling slowly, she made a conscious effort to loosen her grip on the water bottle and her shoes.

When did you lose control of this meeting? Make your point and leave.

"We need a strategy for our interviews. It's important to hide any tension between us from Octavia Jenkins. She's a small-town reporter with big-city aspirations, and she's willing to dig up dirt when necessary."

His eyes narrowed. "You have dirt?"

Other than a long list of loser dates and an on again, off again relationship with a Dean's client? "Me? No. My life's an open book. You?"

He hesitated. "Not personally."

What did that mean? For the first time she wondered if something or someone besides her had driven Clay from Wilmington. But no. She had to go with the facts as she knew them. Clay's mother might buy the story that he'd left home because he couldn't get along with his father, but Andrea didn't believe it for one second. The Dean men had argued hard and often. Everyone claimed it was because they were too much alike. But their bond had been strong despite the bickering.

Clay drank from his bottle and then wiped the back of his hand over his mouth. "Andrea, we were lovers. If Jenkins is as ambitious as you said, she's not going to have to do much digging to uncover that."

"No. But it's not like that's news to anyone who matters."

Pensive furrows carved his brow and a nerve twitched beside his mouth. "How aggressive is she?"

"I don't know. Why?" What kind of secrets did he have?

A shake of his head was her only reply.

Andrea moved away from the computer and glanced down the companionway. Clay's bedroom. Her steps faltered, her pulse quickened and her knees weakened. Why did being ten paces from Clay's berth still get to her? She had no intention of tumbling back into his bed. But an old familiar ache filled her belly.

Nostalgia. That's all it is. Ignore it.

She had to get out of here even though they hadn't settled on a story to feed Octavia Jenkins yet.

"We'll talk later about the reporter. I have a conference call in a few minutes. I'll see you in an hour for the production walk-through."

Clay snapped his cell phone closed and dragged a hand over his face. The pushy journalist had laid waste to his plan to delay the dates as long as possible. If the Miami headhunters found an interim CEO quickly, then he'd have been able to return home without fulfilling his end of the auction bargain.

Cowardly? Probably. But he didn't know if he could date Andrea, spend hours with her by candlelight and firelight and walk away again. No, he wasn't still in love with her, but he was far too attracted to her for his peace of mind. Falling for her again would be too easy. But nothing had changed. In fact, his inability to stick with one woman more than a few months since leaving Andrea reinforced the fact that he might be like his father and incapable of fidelity.

He checked his watch. Damn. Late for his meeting with Andrea. He snatched up the safety glasses required anywhere on the property other than this dock and the sales building and left his yacht behind. Andrea met him at the end of the sidewalk.

How could a woman look attractive in bulky safety glasses and rubber-soled shoes? And yet Andrea did.

Clay shoved on his glasses and cursed his errant hormones. "Sorry to keep you waiting. Phone call. Can you change your plans for tonight?"

Eyes wide, her head whipped toward him. "Why?"

He accompanied her through the security gate and across the pavement toward the first metal building. "Because the reporter is demanding an interview to discuss our first date. That means we need to have one unless you want to blow her off."

"We can't do that." She dipped her head and tugged at her earlobe. Years ago that had been a sign that she was uncomfortable. Was it still?

"I suppose I could." She looked about as excited as she would if he'd invited her to spend the evening in a mosquito-infested swamp without bug repellant.

"The dinner cruise has an opening tonight. Where do you live?"

"I have a house on Wrightsville Beach."

Regret needled him. Eight years ago they'd discussed buying a house on the beach together. "I'll pick you up at seven. The boat sails at seven-thirty. I'll need directions to your place before you leave."

"I'd rather meet you there. That will give both of us more time to get ready."

The door to the building opened before he could reply. Andrea greeted the man and then turned to Clay.

"You remember Peter Stark, don't you? He's our production manager now."

"Good to see you again, Peter." Clay offered his hand. The man hesitated long enough before shaking Clay's hand to make his lack of welcome known without being flagrantly rude.

The cold shoulder shouldn't have surprised Clay but it did. Peter had been Clay's mentor-slash-babysitter from the first day Clay had set foot on Dean's soil. The man's allegiance clearly belonged to Andrea now.

"How's it going, Peter?" Andrea asked.

"Right on schedule except for those cabinets." Peter addressed Andrea. "The fancy wood the owner requested isn't in."

"I'll make a—" Andrea stopped and glanced at Clay as if realizing that would be his job now. "Clay can call the distributor to check status when we get back to the office."

"We could make do with mahogany," Pete insisted.

"My grandfather always said, 'The customer's not paying us to make do. He's paying us to make what he ordered.'" Clay lived by the quote since his clients often made illogical design requests.

"Yeah, well the wood's holding up everything else in line."

"I'll get on it before I leave today. If all else fails, we'll cancel the order and go with my suppliers."

"Your daddy won't like that," Peter challenged. "We've dealt with this company for twenty years."

"My father's not running the show right now. I am. If a company can't deliver, then we'll find one that can—just like our customers will if we don't give them what they've asked for. If the holdup is a problem, then shift the line. Bump the next order in front of this one. I'll make sure the client understands the delay."

The scene repeated itself as they circled the facility and Clay reacquainted himself with familiar faces. Employees addressed Andrea. She redirected them to Clay. By the time they left the building Clay wondered why his mother had begged him to come home. The employees trusted Andrea. They didn't trust him.

Considering he'd left town rather than live a lie or risk failing Andrea the way his father had failed his mother, the lack of trust rubbed salt in an open wound.

Three

If they had to date, then Clay had decided he'd choose the least romantic in the package first. How intimate could a three-hour cruise on a riverboat carrying four hundred people be?

He gave himself a proverbial pat on the back as he followed Andrea and the hostess the length of the brightly lit main salon of the *Georgina* past a laden buffet and tables crowded with families, including boisterous children. Treating this date like a client dinner would be a piece of cake in this setting. They'd probably even have to share a table with strangers.

But instead of showing them to one of the eight-person tables, the hostess stopped in front of a glass-and-brass elevator located at the stern of the ship. They entered the cubicle. Clay caught a glimpse of the second floor as the clear box drifted upward. The lighting on the second level was a little dimmer. A DJ occupied a small stage. Most of the patrons looked like college kids. Nothing he couldn't handle even though he'd given up keg parties years ago.

But the elevator kept rising until it reached the third floor. Clay's stomach sank faster than an anchor. He'd congratulated himself too soon.

The setting sun on the western horizon cast a peachy glow over the upper deck's glass-domed atrium. No more than a dozen widely spaced tables for two occupied the area surrounding a parquet dance floor. At the far end of the enclosure a trio of musicians occupied a small stage.

The doors opened with a ding, and the wail of the sax greeted them. Clay had learned to like jazz during his years at the University of New Orleans, but sultry jazz combined with Andrea in a sexy black dress jeopardized his plan to keep the date on a business footing.

"Mr. Dean?" The hostess held open the doors. Her tone and expression implied it wasn't the first time she'd called him. "I need to seat you. We'll be underway in five minutes."

With a growing sense of unease Clay followed Andrea and the hostess to a table tucked into the far corner. No buffet. No crowds. No noisy kids. No distractions.

Too intimate. He seated Andrea and then himself. The linen-draped table was small enough for him to reach across and hold her hand if he wanted. Which he didn't.

A waitress filled their water goblets, promised to return with champagne and departed.

"Not what you were expecting?" Andrea asked.

How could she still read him after eight years? "I didn't know what to expect. My mother made the arrangements for each date. All I do is choose a day and time." He sipped his water, but the cool liquid stopped short of the burn low in his gut. "The riverboat wasn't here when I left."

"No. She's only been here a few years. The owners brought her in as part of the downtown renewal project."

"There have been a lot of changes." And not just in his hometown.

It should have been impossible for Andrea to look more beautiful tonight than she had in the siren's dress at the auction, but she did. Sunlight sparkled on her loose honey-colored hair, and she'd smudged her eye makeup, giving her a just-out-of bed look that played havoc with his memories. Her silky black wraparound dress swished just above her knees and dipped low between her breasts, hinting at the curves beneath, but revealing nothing except the fact that she wasn't wearing a bra.

He swallowed another gulp of water and wished he hadn't noticed the slight sway beneath the fabric when she'd greeted him at the bottom of the gangplank. But hell, he was a man, and there were some things a guy just couldn't miss. Unrestrained breasts ranked high on that list. His list anyway.

The powerful engines of the riverboat rumbled to life. Clay relished the slight vibration. Some liked the silent glide of sailboats, but he preferred the leashed power and throaty growl of an engine. The boat maneuvered away from the dock and headed up river.

Clay focused on the safe view of the shore rather than the more dangerous one of the woman across from him. The tall pines on the bank were a far cry from the sand, palms and towering waterfront buildings of Miami. He'd become so accustomed to glass, brick and modern construction that he'd forgotten how impressive raw nature could be. The dark green of the treetops and the layers of red and yellow in the riverbank resembled a painting.

The waitress returned, poured the champagne and vanished, leaving a silver ice bucket behind.

Andrea sipped from her flute and stared through the glass at the passing scenery as the sun sank lower. "Wilmington will never be as cosmopolitan as Miami, but it is modernizing."

Clay ignored his champagne. If he hoped to get through tonight without regrets, then he had to keep a clear head. The last thing he needed was alcohol. He rated his chances of avoiding the dance floor and body contact as slim to none. Andrea used to love dancing. She'd even taken ballroom dancing as a physical education class in college.

"Why did you attend the auction?" He forced the question through a constricting throat.

She blinked at his question and hesitated before answering. "Besides the fact that your mother and Juliana's were the event organizers and Holly, Juliana and I were informed that our attendance was mandatory?"

He'd suspected his mother's part in this fiasco would come up eventually. Had she put Andrea up to this? It seemed likely. His mother had adored Andrea, but if Mom was matchmaking, then she was doomed to disappointment. "Yes. Besides that."

Andrea shrugged, drawing his attention to her bare, lightly tanned arms and shoulders. The pencil-thin straps of her dress didn't cover nearly enough skin. "Holly, Juliana and I each turn thirty this year, and we gain control of our trust funds. We don't need the money because we all work and we're well paid, so we decided to invest some and donate the rest to a good cause. The charity auction seemed like a fun idea."

She'd hung with the same crowd since high school. He'd severed his friendships when he'd left town because he hadn't wanted anyone telling him who Andrea had chosen to replace him. Any one of his buddies would have been eager to fill his shoes. "Your friends bought men, too?"

"Yes. Tell me about your company," she said after the waitress served the salads and departed.

"Seascape recruited me during college. Rod Forrester, the owner and an established yacht designer, wanted someone who could buy him out when he was ready to retire. I signed on as an intern, and he taught me the practical side of the business the University of New Orleans couldn't. Rod retired last year."

Andrea's foot bumped his ankle beneath the tiny table. A spark of need ignited and spiraled up Clay's thigh. "Excuse me. Seascape is doing well?"

"Very. Rod was more open-minded than Dad. I never would have won the awards for innovative design working at Dean Yachts." Bitterness crept into his tone.

For several seconds Andrea's caramel-colored gaze studied him. "Your father's not as close-minded as he used to be."

"I like the changes I've seen. Who should I credit for prying him loose from the tar gluing his feet in the past?"

She shrugged. "Me. I told him we either moved forward or we'd be left behind. It helped when business increased along with our marketing expenditures and in doing so validated my push for change."

His opinion of Andrea climbed another notch—something he couldn't afford. She'd managed to change his father's stubborn mind, something Clay hadn't been able to do. Clay and his father had battled over Clay's "new-fangled" ideas and every suggestion for improvement Clay had made had been dismissed.

The band launched into an up-tempo song and other couples took the floor. Clay did his best to ignore them. He couldn't ignore the subtle sway of Andrea's body as she moved her shoulders to the music. Her gaze drifted toward the dancers several times as she finished her salad.

He felt like a heel. He might resent being forced to participate in the auction, but Andrea had paid big bucks for these dates, and he had no right to cheat her. She deserved to get something for her money. Dancing with her would be tough, but he could handle it. He squared his shoulders and stood.

"Shall we?"

Andrea's head tipped back and her hair cascaded over her shoulders. Eyes wide, she dampened her parted lips. Heat unfurled in Clay's belly, and he regretted his invitation, but it was too late to retract it. Andrea's fingers curled around his. Awareness traveled up his arm like a mild electric current.

He led her toward the small parquet square and then he turned, rested one hand on her waist and laced the fingers of his other hand through hers. She stepped into his arms, and *damn,* she fit as if she'd never left.

Her palm burned against his and the heat of her skin permeated the fabric of her dress. He'd forgotten how good she felt in his arms. And he didn't want to remember now. He searched his mind for a diversion. "Tell me about the delivery tomorrow."

"The caterers will arrive to set up at eleven. A champagne luncheon will be served at noon. The party lasts as long as it lasts. At that point the customer calls the shots. Sometimes they board the boat and leave immediately. Sometimes they hang around hours or days while they familiarize themselves with how everything works. Wear a suit tomorrow."

"I remember." He twirled her under his arm. She stepped back into his embrace without missing a beat. Just like old times. Her scent filled his lungs. A strand of her hair snagged on his evening beard. He jerked his head back.

Focus. On. Work. "I haven't had a chance to look at the schedule yet. Who's the client?"

A smile glimmered in her eyes and danced on her lips. "Toby Haynes."

Clay frowned. "The race car driver?"

"Yes. This is his third Dean yacht."

The news that NASCAR's most notorious playboy would be onsite tomorrow distracted Clay from the brush of Andrea's thighs against his, but not enough to stem his reaction to holding her close and knowing only a couple of inches and a few thin pieces of fabric separated him from Andrea's bare skin. He blamed his reaction on abstinence.

He'd broken up with Rena five months ago after she'd thrown a tantrum when he'd given her a sapphire necklace instead of an engagement ring for Christmas. He hadn't misled her because he'd told her up front that he wasn't looking for marriage, but the nasty breakup had left a bitter taste in his mouth. He hadn't dated since. A waiting list of design requests kept his evenings busy. Work was a demanding, but reliable mistress.

Clay glanced at the table. The food—and his excuse for escape—hadn't arrived. "Repeat customers are good."

Andrea's tender smile unsettled him. "Yes and Toby's always fun. He's very hands-on through every stage of production, and since each yacht takes almost a year to complete we see a lot of him. The staff looks forward to his visits."

Had he been hands-on with Andrea? Did she look forward to his visits? An ember in Clay's gut smoldered. *Don't go there, man. You gave up your claim eight years ago.* But he couldn't deny the flicker of jealousy and that pissed him off.

He twirled her again, but Clay wasn't concentrating on his footwork. This time he stepped forward when he should have gone backward. He collided with Andrea. He banded his arms around her to steady her and her soft curves molded against him. His lungs and heart stalled. Every cell in his body snapped to attention. It would be so easy to temporarily forget the demons that had driven him away.

Andrea gasped. Her golden gaze locked with his. Her breath swept his chin. The music played on, but Clay couldn't break free of the magnetic pull to resume the dance. Holding Andrea in his arms felt like coming home.

His lips found hers without him consciously making the decision to kiss her. Sensation sparkled through his veins like a shaken magnum of champagne and his fingers tightened on her waist. His tongue swept over her bottom lip and into the warmth of her mouth. She tasted familiar. How could he remember her flavor after all this time?

She melted into him, meeting him halfway, testing and tangling, stroking. His tongue. His back. His memory. She matched him kiss for passionate kiss, and damn, she tasted good. Silky, sweet and hot, with a hint of champagne. A groan rumbled from his chest as hunger overpowered him.

Her palms splayed on his back under his jacket. The rasp of her nails hit him like a match to dry kindling, inflaming him. He cupped her hips, pulling her even closer. A roar filled his ears. His pulse? The wind?

Applause.

Clay jerked back. The couples around them clapped as the band finished a song, but several diners aimed their indulgent smiles in Clay and Andrea's direction.

Dammit. Dammit. Dammit. Coming home was a

mistake. He couldn't erase the past, and he sure as hell didn't want to revisit it.

He'd never survive ripping his heart out a second time.

Oh God, I'm not over him.

Yes, you are. Andrea silently argued with the voice in her head. Her hormones remembered. That's all.

She was *over* Clayton Dean.

Totally.

She stepped back, mentally and physically separating herself from the man and the memories swamping her. At the same time she filed away the information that her libido had only been hibernating. Good to know since she'd feared that switch had been permanently flipped into the off position.

Battling light-headedness and a racing pulse, she took a shaky breath and fought the urge to cover her hot cheeks. Instead, she hid her clenched fists in the full skirt of her dress. "Our dinner is waiting."

Clay's closed expression revealed nothing. He gestured for her to precede him to the table. Andrea crossed the room on unsteady legs.

One day. One blasted day and already her plan had sprung a leak. Where had she gone wrong? She condemned her traitorous body for ignoring her carefully mapped out plans. She was supposed to make Clay want her not vice versa, but there was no denying the fizz in her blood or the flush on her skin, and her reaction had nothing to do with the champagne in her glass.

Falling for Clay was a dead end street she refused to travel again. If he expected to temporarily resume the physical relationship they'd shared eight years ago, then he was ringing the wrong bell. *Temporary* had been excised from her vocabulary. She wanted forever this time. But not with Clay. She'd never trust his promises again.

As she slid into her chair she blinked in surprise. When had the tiny white lights outlining the frame of the atrium been turned on? She'd been too caught up in Clay to notice. The twinkling bulbs gave the impression of dining beneath a starlit sky. Romantic. Too romantic. But escape from the boat was impossible since they were somewhere in the middle of the Cape Fear River, and hurling herself over-board wouldn't be wise.

She surreptitiously checked her watch. Two more hours to get through. Determined to devote her full attention to her prime rib, she draped her napkin across her lap.

"Should I apologize?"

The huskily voiced question made her heart stumble. She lifted her head with a jerk. Regret filled Clay's deep blue eyes, and for some stupid reason that stung.

Had she expected him to suddenly realize he'd made a mistake by leaving her and declare his undying love? Of course not. She wanted closure, not a new beginning. She needed a man she could count on, one who wouldn't let her down. Clay had abandoned his responsibilities *and her* without looking back.

She forced a smile to her lips and a lightness she didn't feel into her voice. "Apologize for a kiss? Heavens no, Clay. We've shared hundreds of those in the past. But we work together now, so no more of that, okay?"

Clay excelled at running. And he hated himself for it. Not the physical sport which kept him in shape, but the mental gymnastics of avoiding a confrontation that could lead to nothing but trouble.

His feet pounded the pavement as his brain hammered

out the issue. This morning he'd run from Dean Yachts, from Andrea standing alone on the back deck of the sales office with a mug in her hands and her face turned toward the sunrise. He'd run from memories of the countless sunrises they'd shared on the deck of his old sloop and an aching need to spend more with her. He'd run from her casual dismissal of a kiss that had capsized him.

His burning lungs and the sweat pouring from his body told him he'd pushed himself too hard. Circling back, he made it halfway up the Dean driveway before the *thwump, thwump* of an approaching helicopter broke the morning silence. The craft swept over his head, aiming for the helipad beside the sales building—another new addition in the past eight years. Who could it be? Their customer wasn't due for four more hours.

Clay reached the parking lot as three male passengers, each carrying duffel bags, jumped from the helicopter. One waved and Andrea, still on the deck of the sales building, waved back. Even from a hundred yards Clay couldn't miss the smile covering her face. She used to smile that way for him. The thought sucker punched him.

"Andi!" the waving visitor called loud enough to be heard over the rotors and Clay grimaced. The guy must not know how much she hated the nickname, but Andrea's grin widened and she headed toward the helipad.

Clay picked up his pace.

Andrea met the visitors halfway across the lawn. The man leading the pack dropped his bag, snatched her into a hug and swung her off the ground, and then he planted a kiss right on Andrea's smiling lips.

Clay's steps faltered. His lungs weren't the only thing burning. His stomach joined in the party with jealousy he had no right to feel. Andrea wasn't his. Could never be his again.

And then he recognized their guests and the blowtorch in his gut intensified. Toby Haynes and his entourage.

With the NASCAR pretty boy's arm still looped around her waist, Andrea greeted each of the other men and then turned toward the offices. She spotted Clay and her smile faded.

Clay closed the distance between them as the helicopter lifted off. Once the noise and wind died down Andrea said, "Clay, meet Toby Haynes, Bill Riley, his captain, and Stu Cane, his first mate. Gentlemen, this is Clayton Dean. He'll be filling in for his father today."

Haynes sized him up and offered a handshake. "Hey, man. How is your dad?"

Clay's stiffening muscles had nothing to do with his run. He didn't like the guy coiled around Andrea like a boa constrictor. And he didn't know the answer to Haynes's question.

Andrea filled the breach. "Joseph is recovering nicely. He's sorry he can't make it today, but he'll call later if Patricia will let him near a phone. She's trying to keep him from getting entangled with work. He's only allowed one phone call per day."

Clay's belly sank lower. His father had called every day since Clay arrived, and Clay had refused to take his calls.

"I look forward to hearing from Joe," Haynes said. "Won't be the same without him here."

What was with this guy and nicknames? No one called his father Joe.

"You're early." Clay ground out the words. Where had his famed diplomacy gone? Rod had sworn Clay had the coolest head in a crisis of anyone he'd ever worked with. The cool head wasn't in evidence today.

Haynes's smile didn't waver. "Couldn't stay away. Had to see my lady. Lucky I didn't come a'knockin' last night when we got in." He punctuated the statement by squeezing Andrea.

His lady? Did Haynes mean the boat or Andrea? Could be either since boats were referred to as female.

The driver nodded toward the dock. "So whose sweet baby is that in the slip behind *Checkered Flag 3?*"

"Mine," Clay replied through a clenched jaw.

"She's a beaut. Wanna show her off?"

Like he wanted a case of jock itch, but Clay's designs were his business. Personal likes and dislikes didn't enter into it. "Let me take a shower first."

"No need to pretty up on my account, Dean."

Andrea stood between them, her head following the byplay like a fan at a tennis match. Wariness and something Clay couldn't identify filled her eyes. "Toby, I still have loads to do. You guys can wait inside, or I can call Peter to give you a tour of *Checkered Flag 3.*"

Clay would be damned if he'd let Haynes slobber over Andrea for the next four hours. "I'll take care of our customers."

Had he stressed the word *customer* too much?

"See there, angel. Dean junior has us covered. Do your thing, but don't you pretty up either. My eyes couldn't handle it if you were any more gorgeous."

Clay's jaw ached from gritting his teeth. Surely Andrea didn't buy this good ol' boy garbage?

"I'd love a tour, Dean. Starting with your boat. Then mine."

Clay swallowed the emotions boiling inside him. *He's a client.* "You look like a man who'd appreciate a high-performance yacht. Come on board."

Haynes kept pace beside him. His flunkies followed like ducks in a row. "Good lookin' lady."

Clay suspected Haynes meant Andrea—not a discussion

he intended to have. Not until he figured out what in the hell he was going to do with his gut-knotting reaction to Haynes touching her, kissing her. "My best design yet. She was built by a firm in Key West."

He rattled off the boat's specs as he gave his unwanted visitors a guided tour of the inside and then the outside. When they reached the bow Haynes tapped the waist-high fiberglass housing. "What's this?"

"My bike." Clay rocked back the white domed cover to reveal his Harley. He'd bought the motorcycle to celebrate buying out Rod. "I use a hydraulic davit to put her ashore."

Haynes ran his hands over the housing, the wench and motorcycle, caressing each like he would a woman. Not a thought Clay wanted to entertain. "Hot damn. Can my boat be outfitted for one of these?"

"Sure."

"How fast?"

"I'd have to check with the production team, and we'd need the specs for your bike. It's a custom-fitted housing."

"I have a couple of weeks. I scheduled to take that time off to be with Andi anyway." Clay's muscles seized. "I want you on the design team of my next boat. Your design and Dean's quality will make for one sweet baby."

Clay wouldn't be here, but there wasn't any point in revealing that detail. He secured his bike. He wanted this racing redneck off his boat before he knocked him over the rails. "Make yourself at home and help yourself to whatever's in the galley. After I shower I'll call Pete to see if we can accommodate your schedule."

Haynes waited for the other men to circle the starboard and then he turned and stopped, blocking Clay's path. "She's a special lady."

"I'm happy with *The Expatriate*."

"I meant Andrea."

Clay remained silent. It wasn't easy.

"But some bozo hurt her a while back, so she's gun-shy."

An iron fist crushed Clay's heart. "That bozo was me."

Haynes smirked. "I know. Most of your employees have been here a *l-o-n-g* time. They saw how you hurt her and they're real protective of her. None of 'em is shy about warning a fella off." The race car driver's smile turned predatory. "Don't set your heart on taking up where you left off, Dean. I've been coaxing Andi for three years, and I don't aim to lose this race. She will be mine."

Clay's hackles rose at the challenge, but at the same time regret weighted him like ballast for the embarrassment he'd caused Andrea. She'd been working at Dean for a year when he'd left her, and they'd made no secret of their love before that. The employees knew he'd planned to marry her and that he hadn't.

But what in the hell was he supposed to do? He couldn't stand in the front of a church and promise to keep only unto Andrea till death do us part knowing that in the pews behind him sat two people who'd made a mockery of those vows and everything he believed in. If his parents' "perfect" marriage was a lie, then in what could he trust?

Staying in Wilmington had meant either lying for his father and concealing the affair, or revealing the sordid truth and breaking the hearts of the two women he loved the most—his mother and Andrea. So he'd run, because taking the dirty secret and leaving town would hurt both women less in the long run than his father's and her mother's betrayal would.

No, Clay realized, he couldn't have Andrea, but he'd be damned if he'd let this race car Romeo hurt her. From what he'd read in his sports magazines Haynes didn't park his car in anybody's garage long-term. He only made pit stops.

Andrea deserved a man who'd love her forever.

"If you haven't won her by now, Haynes, then you don't have what it takes. It's time for you to haul your car to another track."

Four

Sandwiched between the man she'd once loved and the man she thought she could love, Andrea struggled to keep her hands and voice steady.

This was her first yacht delivery without Joseph, and her mentor was counting on her to get it right. She wouldn't let him down. Thank heavens most of the work had been done ahead of time, because concentrating on the details of the celebration was nearly impossible under the circumstances.

How could she focus on her speech or the presentation of the flag signed by every employee who'd worked on Toby's boat with Clay glued to her side? Could he possibly stand any closer? Moving away didn't work because he shadowed her. His cologne, a refreshing blend of lime and sandalwood, permeated every breath she took. Their hands and hips bumped *again,* and her pulse stuttered just as it had the last dozen times.

And how could she help but compare the two men when Toby seemed determined to shoehorn himself between her and Clay? Both men were lean, muscular and just over six feet tall, but there the similarities ended. Clay's beaver-brown hair and blue eyes were shades darker than Toby's sandy hair and silvery eyes.

Toby was serious about his driving, but little else. He was always good for a laugh and a good time. Whereas Clay—the new Clay—seemed serious about everything. Where had his easy and seductive smiles gone? Not that she wanted to be seduced, but the intense way he looked at her now made her skin feel dry and other places…well, the opposite.

Damn. It. Attraction toward Clay was not part of her plan.

Her feelings for each of the men were so different. She'd loved Clay blindly and without reservation—the way only the young can. Her feelings for Toby on the other hand were more mature, more cautious. She accepted that he wasn't perfect, and he seemed willing to accept what she was willing to give. Not that she'd given him much yet.

While both Clay and Toby smiled and sounded courteous as they discussed elements of the yacht and the features Toby wanted Clay to add, there was an underlying tension crackling between them. They clearly didn't like each other, but why? Andrea looked from one man to the other, searching for clues.

As if he took her scrutiny as a sign of encouragement, Toby hooked an arm around her hip, pulling her away from Clay. He clinked his champagne flute against hers and then leaned closer.

"With Junior here to handle the company you can take your vacation after all, Andi." He didn't speak as quietly or intimately as she would have expected considering their foreheads touched. "I'm leaving the boat here so your boys can add a few more toys to it, but you and I can fly down to the Bahamas, party all night and stay in bed all day."

Andrea's mouth dried and her heart raced, but not with the anticipation she'd expected to feel. She didn't dare look over her shoulder to see what Clay thought of Toby's invitation. He had to have heard it as did everyone else in the vicinity.

A confusing swirl of emotions whipped through her. Toby was attractive, the poster boy of the NASCAR circuit, and when he kissed her she felt...*something*. Not explosions, but his kisses were pleasantly stimulating. Months ago she'd accepted his invitation to spend the two weeks after he took possession of his yacht cruising with him because she thought they could have a future together. They weren't lovers yet, but if Joseph hadn't had a stroke that would have changed tonight.

"Andrea is needed here," Clay said in an authoritative tone that rubbed Andrea like coarse grit sandpaper and snapped her to rigid attention.

She had no intention of leaving town. In fact, as soon as she'd heard Joseph's prognosis she'd called Toby and informed him that she needed to cancel because she couldn't leave Dean in limbo. But to have Clay demand she stay... Indignation flushed her skin. Couldn't he have asked?

She considered arguing just for the sake of arguing, but she wasn't going to leave, so what was the point? With her mind in turmoil over Clay's return and the lingering attraction she felt for him, she didn't want to commit to an intimate relationship with Toby at the moment. She refused to go to bed with one man when another monopolized most of her waking and sleeping thoughts.

She had to exorcise Clay before she could move

forward. Besides, she'd yet to accomplish any of the tasks she'd set for herself when she decided to buy him.

"Would you excuse us a moment, Toby?" She grabbed Clay's bicep, and his muscles flexed beneath her fingers. His body heat burned her palm through his silk shirt. It took an inordinate amount of concentration on her footing to lead him to the far corner of the reception hall without mishap because her leg muscles wanted to turn mushy. The moment she arrived she removed her hand and shifted her cool champagne glass to her hot palm. "My vacation has been scheduled for months. If I wanted to take it, I could."

"I would think your priorities have changed. Where's your allegiance to my father?"

"Where's yours?" How dare *he* question her dedication?

Anger darkened Clay's eyes and flattened his lips. "I'm here, aren't I?"

And eager to leave as soon as possible. The perfect solution popped into her brain. She leaned back on her heels and smiled. "I'll postpone my vacation if you'll call off your headhunters. Stay until Joseph's back on his feet and I'll do the same."

A nerve in Clay's jaw jumped. His nostrils flared. "You didn't used to be manipulative."

"I didn't have to be. Everything I wanted was mine for the asking." And now it wasn't. Not that she wanted to go back to being the spoiled girl she used to be. She'd found immense satisfaction in earning her rewards instead of having everything handed to her.

Clay's gaze swept the room and then seemingly focused on Toby. "You have yourself a deal. I'll stay, but don't forget we have the interview with that reporter you want to impress Thursday night and six more dates. Make sure you're available."

"I will be. Excuse me." Andrea returned to Toby. She could feel Clay right behind her. "I'm needed here while Joseph's out of commission, but I'll hold you to the rain check you promised."

Toby winked. "Gonna let me bunk at your place since you were gonna be bunking in mine?"

Clay stepped into her line of vision—one long, lean line of tense male. Disapproval radiated off him in waves. Why? There were no rules in the employee handbook prohibiting fraternization between staff and customers. She frowned at him and then, forcing a smile to her lips, turned back to Toby.

"And have you miss spending the first night on your new yacht? I wouldn't dream of it. Besides, *Checkered Flag 3* is stocked and ready to go. You and the guys can stay on board and eat some of that food. The Dean's crew will work around you."

Toby touched her cheek. "Then at least let me take you to dinner."

Clay's hand settled on her waist, startling her. "You can have her tonight, but tomorrow night she's mine. I guess Andrea forgot to mention she bought me and seven dates with me at a bachelor auction. We have another date tomorrow night."

And that's when understanding clicked into place. She was a bone and she'd just been pitched into a dog fight. But that made absolutely no sense because Clay didn't want her, a fact his eagerness to leave town made clear. So what was his problem?

Grouchier than hell from a lack of sleep, Clay paused his warm-up stretches the moment Andrea stepped out on the back deck of the sales building with a mug in her hand.

Her morning ritual, he'd discovered, included arriving an hour before the gates opened and sitting on the deck to enjoy the sunrise.

The sense of relief he felt that she hadn't spent the night on Haynes's boat only worsened Clay's foul mood. He had no business caring where she slept or with whom. But he did care, dammit. He wanted her to be happy, and a race car driver with a short attention span and a bad track record wasn't going to do the job.

He grabbed his water bottle and his shirt, and then vaulted from his deck to the dock and headed in her direction. His unrested muscles protested the move. He'd spent half the night tossing and turning, involuntarily listening for Haynes to return from his dinner date and wondering if Andrea would be "bunking" with the cocky jackass.

Each slap of the windswept waves against the bulkhead had reminded Clay of the days and nights he and Andrea had spent in the narrow berth of his sloop. Because both of them lived at home when they weren't sharing university dorm rooms with other students, privacy had been scarce and most of their lovemaking had taken place in the tiny airless cabin of his sailboat.

Did she ever think about the hot summer days and nights when they'd made love until sweat puddled on their skin?

Last night he couldn't think about anything else, and when he'd fallen asleep Technicolor reruns had streamed through his dreams.

"How's the view from your place?" he called out.

She spun abruptly in his direction. Another one of those curve-hugging suits outlined her figure, this one in a pale pink color that brought out the flush on her cheeks. The above the knee length of her skirt combined with a pair of dangerously high heels made her legs look seriously sexy. His pulse slapped like a flag in a gale force wind.

"Pardon me?"

Andrea had always had a thing about killer shoes. From what he'd observed that hadn't changed. With Herculean effort he winched his gaze upward over her legs, hips, narrow waist, breasts, raspberry lips and eventually reached her golden brown eyes.

"You're still hooked on sunrises. I'm guessing you bought your beach house for the view."

She sipped from her mug. Coffee, he guessed, from the scent mingling with her perfume on the morning air. "Good guess. And it's lovely, but not as peaceful as here."

The sweep of her hand encompassed a fish jumping, an egret taking flight from the opposite bank and a family of otters playing nearby. Her gaze coasted over his bare chest, down his torso and then his legs, making him damned glad he'd installed a home gym on *The Expatriate*. He tightened his fingers on the T-shirt he carried and hoped his thin running shorts would conceal his body's instantaneous reaction to her proximity. He'd been hard all night with no relief. Was it any surprise he'd spring eagerly back into action?

"Late night?" Haynes hadn't returned until two. Had he been with Andrea the entire time?

"That's none of your business, Clay, unless it affects my work."

"It is if you fall asleep on me. I've set up another date for this evening. We're going horseback riding on Holden Beach before meeting with Octavia Jenkins. I'll pick you up at six."

"No need. We can leave from here."

"What? You don't want me in your house?"

She hesitated a beat too long. "Not at all. My house

would be out of the way. I keep a set of casual clothes in my office."

He wanted to see her house, wanted to know if she'd built the one she'd planned so many years ago. He opened his mouth to insist on picking her up, but a wolf whistle from the dock interrupted. Clay didn't have to turn to know Haynes was awake.

"Don't let me keep you from your run, Clay," Andrea said, but her gaze and smile were directed at the car jockey.

Dismissed and pissed. Wasn't that a great way to start his day?

One more date down and her heart none the worse off, Andrea congratulated herself on Wednesday evening as she approached the parking area beside the stable where she and Clay had borrowed horses for their sunset ride on Holden Beach.

Screeching gulls, crashing surf and thundering hooves had made talking difficult, and since each of them had their own mounts there had been no touching and no sparks. Well, relatively no sparks.

She'd experienced a few flickers when a sexy motorcyclist wearing low-slung jeans, a snug white T-shirt and boots had pulled up beside her car in the gravel lot. She couldn't help checking out his wide-shouldered, lean-hipped, tight-butted form as he climbed from his bike, but then he'd removed his helmet and her stomach had hit rock bottom. Clay.

Because of Toby's upgrade request she'd known Clay owned a motorcycle, but she hadn't seen Clay's bike and her brain hadn't merged the pictures of Clay and a Harley. It was a sexy visual she could live very well without.

He'd breached her defenses twice today. This morning

he'd gotten to her with his bare, hair-dusted chest, six pack abs and skimpy running shorts. Not good. Not good at all. But this evening's sparks didn't count, did they, since she hadn't known who caused them until it was too late to douse them?

She spotted Octavia Jenkins waiting at the head of the trail and slowed her steps.

"Evening, folks," the reporter said. "I thought we'd do the interview right over there at the picnic table. I've already lit a couple of citronella candles to keep the mosquitoes away."

This is where they would find out how much of the past the reporter intended to rake up. Hoping Octavia would keep her article light and entertaining, Andrea crossed the wiry grass with dread weighting her feet. She sat at the table and Clay settled across from her. Their feet bumped beneath the scarred wood and her heart hiccupped.

No more of that.

Octavia flipped open her notebook and then turned to Andrea. "Is it difficult to work for a man you once thought you'd marry?"

Andrea froze with her hand midsweep through her tangled hair. So much for light and fun. She fought the urge to squirm on the bench of the picnic table, and she didn't dare look at Clay. "Th-that was a long time ago. Both Clay and I are more concerned with Joseph's rehabilitation and maintaining Dean's production schedule than we are with our former relationship."

"Any chance of fanning those old embers back to life?"

"No," Andrea and Clay answered quickly and simultaneously.

Andrea sought his gaze across the table, but his narrowed gaze focused on the reporter. She knew *she* was lying about the unexpected remnants of attraction, but was Clay? Had he been completely unmoved by Monday night's kiss?

And what about this morning? He'd practically undressed her with his eyes—a pulse pounding event for her. Damn. It. Had it had any effect on him?

"You're barking up the wrong tree," Clay added as if he'd guessed her question, and Andrea's cheeks burned.

"I could swear I've seen a few smoke signals." Octavia paused to write something in her notebook. Andrea wished she could read what it said, but the flickering candle didn't provide enough light in the shadowy dusk to make it possible to read anything from her side of the table.

"You started dating your senior year in high school. According to your yearbook, your class voted you most inseparable couple, most likely to have a dozen kids and most likely to celebrate your fiftieth wedding anniversary together. The fact that you dated for five years after graduation despite attending universities a thousand miles apart supports your schoolmates' predictions. How could they be so wrong?"

Ohgodohgodohgod. Andrea's gaze found Clay's. *Please don't reveal my biggest flaw—whatever it is—to this reporter.*

"People and circumstances change," Clay said quietly with his gaze locked on Andrea's.

His answer both relieved and frustrated her. She wanted to know why he'd left, but she didn't want *the world*, or even the readers of the Wilmington newspaper, to know.

Octavia wrote and then looked up. "How does it feel to return to the job that was destined to be yours, Clay?"

"My life and my design firm are in Florida now. This is temporary." Tension clipped his words.

"Do you like your new company better than being part of a sixty-year-old family business your grandfather founded?"

Andrea didn't envy Clay being on the hot seat, but she secretly applauded Octavia for asking the very questions that had run through her own mind.

"It's neither better nor worse. I saw an opportunity and took it."

The reporter persisted. "I'm just trying to understand what made you decide to chuck a guaranteed future. You are the only heir to the Dean Yachts' fortune. What will happen to the company and its employees once your father's gone? Will the company fold, be sold or will you take over?"

The shift of Clay's jaw and the tightening of his fist on the table signaled his uneasiness. Andrea found herself feeling sympathy for Clay instead of the antipathy she should be feeling. She should relish his discomfort, but instead she wanted to reach out to him. Since the reporter would definitely get the wrong idea if she did, Andrea stretched her leg beneath the table and brushed her foot against Clay's booted ankle. It was something they used to do at family dinners, a way to stay connected when circumstances demanded otherwise.

Other than a flicker of his eyelids Clay didn't acknowledge her touch, but warmth tingled up Andrea's leg.

Get a grip. Your shoe touched his boot.

Maybe she didn't have any effect on him anymore. If that were the case, then making him regret what he'd given up would be a lost cause. No. She couldn't believe a relationship that had turned her life inside out had left him totally unscathed. She'd continue to wear her sexiest suits and her look-at-me shoes.

Eat your heart out, Clayton Dean.

She faced Octavia. "That decision is years down the road. Joseph's stroke was minor. He's on medications to prevent another one and he should be fine. Certainly, he'd like for Clay to come home, but he understands Clay's need to prove himself."

Clay's gaze found and searched hers as though asking if what she said was true. Andrea gave a slight nod.

If Joseph Dean knew why Clay had left town, he had never said. But one thing Andrea knew for certain was that Joseph, although saddened by Clay's abrupt departure, had never condemned his son. His lack of anger convinced Andrea beyond a shadow of doubt that the problem that had driven Clay from town was her. Otherwise, Joseph, who liked to vent, would have spouted off long and hard over Clay's desertion.

"Your father is on line two," Fran said Friday morning through the wireless intercom-slash-phone system the crew had rigged up for Clay to use in his dockside office.

Clay's heart slammed against his chest like a boat hitting a sandbar at full throttle. For the past two days the reporter's question had echoed in his head. "What will happen once your father's gone? Will the company fold, be sold or will you take over?"

How could he walk away from the dream his grandfather had worked so hard to make a reality—a dream Clay had shared for many years? How could he not?

Hell, he couldn't even face going into the offices. Since Wednesday night he'd avoided Andrea whenever possible and used the phone or e-mail to communicate instead of walking the short distance up the dock to the offices. Seeing the sympathy in her eyes after the way he'd treated her had hit him hard.

From the safety of Miami nearly eight hundred miles away he'd underestimated the difficulty of being near her and not touching her. The physical attraction hadn't died.

If anything, he found the mature and confident Andrea more potent than the girl he'd left behind.

"Mr. Dean?"

Clay reached for the button to tell Fran he wasn't available—the way he had every other time his father called. But that wouldn't stop the calls. "I'll take it," he said and lifted the receiver.

"You need to stop wasting your one phone call a day on me. I have nothing to say to you," he said to his father without preamble.

"Clayton. Son. We need to talk."

He hadn't heard his father's voice in eight years. It didn't resonate like it used to. The words sounded slow and measured. A trick of his memory or a result of the stroke? Clay hardened his heart.

"You said all you needed to say when you asked me to lie for you."

"I regret that. I was wrong."

"No kidding." Sarcasm sharpened his tone. "And there were two of you. Two of you who swore that you had perfect marriages. Marriages between high school sweethearts. Just like Andrea and me. It was a lie."

"I never cheated before or since, son. I swear it."

Acid burned Clay's throat. "You expect me to believe you?"

"I told your mother I'd been unfaithful. She forgave me, Clay. Can't you?"

"Did you tell her you cheated with her best friend? With a woman she loved like a sister?"

Silence stretched between them. "No. I risked a twenty-five-year marriage by coming clean. I didn't want to ruin her lifetime friendship with Elaine. There were extenuating circumstances—"

"So you're still living a lie."

"I've accepted responsibility for my actions. Now you need to take responsibility for yours. You shouldn't have made Andrea suffer for my mistake. You had no right to hurt that girl, Clay. My weakness had nothing to do with her."

A familiar stab of pain hit him. No, his father's weakness had nothing to do with Andrea and everything to do with Clay. Everyone called Clay a chip off the old block. Was his father's inability to be faithful a flaw Clay had inherited? He hadn't wanted to risk it. Hell, he'd been afraid to.

"You have no business telling me what's right."

"Clay, there's something you need to know."

"I don't want to hear any more of your confessions or your excuses."

"And I'm not offering them. Please, son, I wouldn't ask if it weren't important. Give me a few minutes of your time."

"I'm giving you and Dean Yachts two months of my life. Don't get greedy and don't call again." And then he replaced the receiver.

"What are you doing on board?"

Andrea gasped and pivoted toward the door of the stateroom. She hadn't heard Clay approach over the sound of the yacht's engine, the clap of water against the hull and the crew members bellowing back and forth above deck as they tested various mechanics of the yacht they were about to put through its paces. If all went well, the craft would be ready for pickup next week.

"I'm helping with the sea trial. Why are you here?"

"Overseeing the trial. You don't need to come along."

"Your father asked me to."

Clay folded his arms across his chest, straining his butter-colored polo shirt at the shoulder seams. The color picked up the sun-bleached highlights in his hair. His khaki-covered legs splayed in the doorway. "I'll handle it."

"Will you call Joseph and report back? He'll want to hear every detail."

"Stark will call him."

"If all your father wanted was Peter's report, I'd fax it to him. Joseph wants to be here. He's never missed a trial. And since he can't be here he wants a firsthand accounting. From me. So you can go back to your office and do whatever it is you do when you hide in there all day."

"I'm not hiding. I'm avoiding the nauseating cow eyes you're making at Haynes."

"Cow eyes! I'm doing no such thing. I go to lunch and dinner with Toby. That's it. I do not make stupid faces." How could she when she was totally conscious of Clay acting like a wet-blanket chaperone just one slip down the dock?

"If you leave now, you can have lunch with him today."

"Forget it, Clay. I'm not getting off this boat. I made a promise and I keep *my* promises."

Clay's lips tightened and his nostrils flared. His hands fell to his side and he clenched his fists. From the hard glint in his eyes she guessed he wasn't thinking about her promise to his father, but the promise Clay had broken eight years ago.

She wished the words back. This wasn't a discussion she wanted to have when any of the three crew members aloft could and probably would interrupt them at any moment since the boat had to be inspected from bow to stern.

"If you'll excuse me, I need a copy of the checklist." She tried to brush past him, but he remained planted like a bulkhead in her path. The horn sounded, signaling that they were pulling away from the dock, and then the boat moved beneath her feet.

"Andrea, I had to leave."

She checked the companionway past his shoulder. Empty.

"Really? And you couldn't have taken the time to say goodbye in person? You had to leave a message on my home phone at a time when you knew I'd be sitting at my desk at work? 'Andrea, I'm sorry, but I can't marry you. I'm leaving town and I won't be back. Forget about me.'" She mimicked his voice and hated that hers cracked over the last phrase. She hated even more that she could still remember the exact words he'd used to dump her.

He grimaced and swallowed, looking very much like a man in pain, but if he felt pain or anything else over breaking her heart, he'd erased it from his eyes by the time he lifted his lids. "It's the best I could do at the time."

Aggravation gurgled in her throat. "If you want me to understand why you were such an inconsiderate ass, then you're going to have to do better than that, Clay."

"I'm sorry."

"I don't want an apology. I want an explanation."

He held her gaze and then shook his head. "An apology is all I'm offering."

"That's not good enough." She tried to step around him, but he caught her upper arms, pushed her back a step and kicked the door closed.

Oh hell. Ready or not, it looked like they were going to duke this out now.

Five

Clay's thumbs stroked the sensitive skin on the insides of Andrea's arms and a telling shiver rushed over her. Damn. It. She did not want him to know he could still get to her.

"Do you think I didn't hate hurting you? Leaving you?"

"Then why did you?"

His silence cut deep. "I couldn't... I couldn't stay."

His hoarse words cut deeper. She gathered her damaged dignity and tried in vain to shake off his tight, but not painful grip. "I'm glad you found it so easy to move on with your life and forget about us. Now let me out of this cabin."

"Listen."

"Let me go, Clay. The crew—"

"Do you hear that?"

All she heard were the sounds of a boat underway and her pulse hammering in her ears. "Hear what?"

"The waves breaking against the hull. Every time I

hear it I think about us on *Sea Scout*. Hot. Sweaty. Naked."

Not fair. Desire exploded inside her, radiating outward until Andrea's skin flushed with the memory of making love on Clay's boat. The fight drained out of her. "Don't you dare bring up that."

"I didn't forget, Andrea." His hands slid upward, over her shoulders and her neck until he cupped her jaw. Andrea stood frozen in his grasp and yet something deep inside her melted. This was so not part of her pla—

His lips touched hers and her objections sputtered into silence. Soft sips turned into hungry, consuming, tongue-entwining kisses as he coaxed her into responding. His fingers threaded through her hair, tilting her head back and holding her as his lips slanted left and then right, always delving deeper.

Her fists bunched by her side and then she lifted them and clutched his waist. She meant to push him away. Really, she did. But she needed to hold on. For balance. Either the boat had hit turbulence or she had.

He shifted his stance and her breasts brushed his chest. Daggers of desire slashed through her, carving a trail to her womb. She'd forgotten how marvelous the tightening coil of arousal felt. Forgotten the steam of Clay's breath against her cheek, the rasp of his afternoon beard on her chin and the bite of hunger so strong she could barely think.

Why could no other man do this to her?

His hands raked down her spine to splay over her bottom, caressing, heating, arousing, and then he drew her closer and the rigid press of his erection burned her belly.

He wasn't unaffected by this *thing* between them. Good to know. She rose on her toes, wound her arms around him and leaned against him, fusing her body to the length of his. He traced her hip, her waist, her ribs and then one big hand opened over her breast, molding her. The lightweight fabric of her sleeveless sheath dress offered no protection from the warmth of his touch. His thumb grazed her nipple, circling, scraping until a needy sound squeaked past her lips and into his mouth. She broke the kiss to gasp for breath.

His mouth found her throat. Nipped. Suckled. Laved. He urged her backward until the berth hit the back of her legs and his thigh wedged between hers. Sweet pressure. Agonizing friction. Her nails dragged down his back and his groan rattled against her.

So delicious. So not part of her plan.

The sound of footsteps penetrated the steamy windows of her brain. She jerked out of Clay's arms and swiped a hand across her mouth a split second before the stateroom door opened.

Peter jolted to a stop, his narrowed eyes taking in the cabin's two heavy breathing occupants. His lips turned down. "We've reached the inlet. I brought copies of the checklist. Clay, we need you above deck. Start in the galley. Sir," he added belatedly.

Andrea's face and neck stung—not only from what she suspected would be a bad case of beard burn.

Clay shot her a look she couldn't decipher, snatched a checklist from Peter's hand and then left.

Andrea exhaled slowly and met the gaze of the man who'd been her staunchest ally at Dean's besides Joseph. The disappointment in Peter's eyes hit hard, but not as harshly as she condemned herself.

Are you out of your mind?
Closure, dummy. That's what you want.
Nothing more. Nothing less.

* * *

What in the hell was he thinking? Clay raked a hand through his hair and leaned against the bulkhead.

Kissing Andrea, holding her had been amazing, but then he'd known it would be. No lover over the past eight years had excited or fulfilled him the way Andrea had. But he couldn't start something with her because he couldn't finish it.

So why torture himself?

Because sitting in his boat every evening and listening to her laughter as she and the car jockey sat on the other yacht's back deck sipping cocktails was torturing him. The only thing worse than their laughter was the silence when they retired inside. Being staked to an anthill would be easier to endure than the silence and wondering if they were in Haynes's hot tub or spread across his king-size bed.

Andrea had called Clay an ass for not dumping her in person, and he couldn't change her opinion by explaining why he'd run from the Dean offices, climbed into his car and driven until an empty gas tank made him pull over. He'd sat on the side of the highway for hours thinking about the repercussions of his discovery and searching for understanding. He'd stayed there until a passing state trooper had pulled in behind him and called a tow truck.

God knows Clay had needed to talk to someone, but who could he have called? He'd trusted no one the way he did Andrea, and he couldn't tell her. He'd left the phone message because he hadn't trusted himself to look her in the eyes or even hear her voice without blurting out the painful truth about their parents and his own doubts.

Could he have committed to one woman forever—the long-distance lover he'd only seen during summers and school vacations for the past five years? Or would he be as weak as his father? Clay would never know. He'd made his choice and he had to live with it.

He checked off the last item on his list and located Andrea and the crew in the salon. "Done."

His pulse accelerated the moment his gaze found hers. He could still feel the heat of her kiss on his lips and the throb of need in his blood. She quickly looked away but not before he saw regret in her eyes.

What if he told her why he'd left? He'd asked himself that question a thousand times. Could she forgive him for spoiling her illusions about her mother and her mentor? Or would she hate him for selfishly ripping the blinders off so they could be together?

And did he even want another chance with her? Giving her up the first time had damned near destroyed him, and he wasn't sure he could go through that again and stay sane. Best to keep his distance as he'd originally planned. No matter how much he wanted her.

"Come about and open her up," Stark told the captain. "Andrea has plans tonight. We don't want to make her late."

Clay's gut muscles clenched. "With Haynes?"

Andrea's chin lifted. "No. With my mother. Not that it's any of your business, but Friday night is girls' night. It's tradition."

A tradition she'd started back in her college days when she'd moved into the dorm room she'd shared with Holly and Juliana, he recalled. She was still close to her mother. That meant Clay definitely had to keep the secret. Better for her to think ill of him. She could find another lover, not one who'd love her as completely as he had, but she couldn't find another mother.

As long as that lover wasn't Haynes.

Clay turned to Stark. "How long before we get that housing built for Haynes's motorcycle?"

"Another week. Had to fabricate a mold." The production manager's disapproval was hard to miss.

"Put a rush on it. We have another delivery next Friday. We need to get his yacht away from the dock ASAP."

"We can move it to another dock. Or you can move yours," Stark said with just a touch of belligerence. Clay almost called him on it, but firing the production manager would only lengthen his stay in Wilmington.

"Get the job done, Peter. Ask for volunteers for extra shifts if you have to."

And in the meantime, Clay decided, he'd keep Andrea occupied by scheduling as many of the auction dates as he could while Haynes was in town.

Both the prodigal son, Clayton Dean, and Andrea Montgomery, the former love of his life, swear the ashes of their past are cold, but this reporter believes this romance is ready to be rekindled. Is Ms. Montgomery carrying the matches? And will Dean Yachts survive the heat when this dynamic duo reignites?

"Oh my God." Andrea groaned, dropped the Saturday newspaper on the kitchen table and buried her face in her hands. Octavia Jenkins's first installment in the Wilmington paper embarrassed Andrea beyond words and made her sick to her stomach. That was nausea twisting her stomach in knots, wasn't it? Of course it was. How would she hold her head up at work?

She lifted her head to peek again at the black-and-white picture of her and Clay sharing a liplock on the *Georgina*.

Who had taken that picture and when? She'd hadn't seen the reporter or photographer on the boat, but then Holly had warned her that Octavia had a sneaky side.

This was all Clay's fault.

Anger propelled her through showering and dressing. She drove like a mad woman to Dean's and practically scorched a trail down the dock past Toby's darkened boat to board Clay's. Lifting her fist, she hammered on the glass upper portion of Clay's door. When Clay didn't respond she pounded harder until she saw a light come on inside and then he emerged from his stateroom. Her stomach flip-flopped. She must have woken him.

Clay jogged up the stairs and across the salon. By the time he unlocked and slid open the door Andrea had worked up a good head of steam. How dare he look so damned sexy with his stubble-shadowed jaw. He also looked rumpled. And bare. And aroused. His wrinkled boxers couldn't conceal his morning erection even in the dim light cast by the lampposts on the dock.

Her entire body warmed. Which only angered her more.

"What's wrong?" he asked.

Andrea blinked away her unwanted response and slapped the newspaper against his chest.

"Read it. Worse, look at the picture. I will not be a pity case again when you leave. Been there. Done that. Didn't like the T-shirt."

Clay wrestled the wrinkled newspaper from her hands, flipped on the overhead light and scanned the article.

Andrea mashed her lips together and fumed. "You have got to stop kissing me."

Clay lifted his gaze. "Stop kissing me back."

"You— I—" she sputtered with fury. Any second now

she was going to shriek like a boiling tea kettle. "How dare you try to blame this on me."

"Aren't you the one wearing figure-hugging suits and do-me heels to work everyday?"

Guilty. Her cheeks caught fire. "I dress to please myself."

"Yeah. Right. Either you're trolling your bait for me or Haynes. Which is it?"

Speechless with rage she glared at him.

He dragged a hand over his bristly chin and her fingers prickled. Damn. It. "Do you know what time it is, Andrea?"

"I—" In her rush to confront Clay she'd forgotten her watch, but the sun had barely begun to lighten the horizon. "No."

"It's 5:20 a.m. Too early to stand in the cockpit and have a screaming match. Come inside. I'll make coffee."

He pivoted and headed for the galley, slinging the paper onto the table as he passed and flicking on lamps. Andrea stood on the deck and debated the intelligence of following him.

For one, Clay wasn't dressed. She risked a peek at his tight tush and then wished she hadn't when her pulse skipped.

For two, he looked too delicious with all that tanned, hair-dusted skin on display. Damn. It.

For three, she hated that she was still attracted to him—so attracted that even Octavia Jenkins could see it. If the reporter could, then who else could? And what would it do to the relationship she planned to have with Toby?

And last, Dean's employees would read this article and think her a fool for falling for him again. She'd lose the respect she'd fought so hard to win.

"Shut the door. You're letting in mosquitoes."

Against her better judgment Andrea stepped over the threshold and closed the door, sealing herself into the intimacy of Clay's salon. It was one thing to conduct business with him when they were both fully dressed, but another when he had pillow creases on his cheek and shoulder.

"This is not the kind of publicity we want, Clay."

"Nope, but what can you do about it? She's writing the story."

"We can stop giving her anything to write about."

Clay punched the on switch and his coffeemaker gurgled to life. "You're the one who insisted we had to go on the dates."

But that was when she had a fail-safe agenda. Now she wasn't so sure her success was guaranteed. But backing out of the auction package would only cause more speculation. "We have to go on the dates. She'd have a field day if we didn't."

"Speaking of dates, I planned to call you today. I've scheduled the hot air balloon ride for five tomorrow morning if you're available." He leaned against the counter and Andrea fought to ignore his nakedness. They'd had countless talks in their past wearing less. Why did the breadth of his shoulders, his six-pack abs, lean hips and long legs still mesmerize her? It wasn't fair. But at least his erection had subsided. Otherwise she wasn't sure she'd be able to locate a functioning brain cell.

Her gaze skimmed back up the dark line of hair dividing his torso and slammed smack dab into Clay's narrowed eyes. He'd caught her checking out his package. Embarrassment heated her like a sauna, making her skin hot and tight.

"I'm available. For the balloon ride. Could you put on some clothes?"

He held her gaze for ten full seconds, and then he pushed off the counter and descended the stairs, but he didn't close his bedroom door. Andrea tried to look away, but her unimpeded view of his stateroom and the corner of his bed covered in tangled sheets captivated her. Coming on the heels of yesterday's kiss and Clay's confession that the sound of water against the hull made him think of her and sex made the air-conditioned interior suddenly feel twenty degrees hotter.

How stupid was she that she couldn't see a train wreck coming and step off the tracks? But she couldn't abandon her mission. She hadn't gotten Clay out of her system, found out why he'd left her, or reunited him with his father. Her job wasn't anywhere near finished. No matter how much she wanted it to be.

"I can't believe I let you talk me into this," Andrea grumbled as she climbed from Clay's rental car in an open field Sunday morning. "Of all the auction dates *this* is the one I dreaded the most."

Clay's smile flashed white in the predawn hours of Sunday morning. "Afraid of heights?"

Andrea looked across the field to where the huge hot air balloon waited like a hulking shadow. There wasn't enough light to make out the colors. The headlights of a van illuminated four people clustered around the balloon basket sitting on the ground. Soon she and Clay would be up—way up—in that. "Maybe. A little. And your package promised sun*sets* not sun*rises*."

"You prefer sunrises."

It touched her that he'd considered her preferences, but a sunrise ascent was too romantic for words, and she didn't want romance from Clay. Especially not after the newspaper article and seeing him practically naked. It was bad enough that his kisses still made her blood simmer. Okay, boil, she admitted, but no more of that.

Her hiking boots and jean clad legs swished in the tall, dew-covered grass as they neared the balloon team's van. She shoved her hands into the pockets of her sweatshirt jacket. "There's no steering wheel and no parachute."

"Hot air balloons have been around since the seventeen hundreds, and our pilot is a licensed twenty-year veteran."

"His experience is the only reason I agreed to this." She'd been asking herself if she was crazy ever since Clay told her about the date yesterday morning.

"Good morning," a man in a flight suit called out. "I'm Owen, your pilot, and these folks are Denise, Larry and Hank, our ground crew. They'll pick us up on the other end and return you to your vehicle. If you're ready to see the world from a bird's-eye view, then climb aboard."

He entered the basket first and then turned to lend Andrea a hand. On unsteady legs she mounted the portable steps the crew provided, climbed inside and clutched the basket's rim. Clay followed. The first thing Andrea noticed was the lack of space. The three foot by four foot basket was crowded with the three of them, a cooler and a couple of metal air tanks. If you weren't friendly with your fellow passengers before you took off, you would be before you landed. The second thing she noted was the proliferation of ropes and cables connecting the basket and balloon and who knew what else. She quickly scanned each line, looking for frays, and thankfully, found none.

"Ready to cast off?" Owen asked.

As tense as an anchor line in a strong current, Andrea nodded. Her heart raced with a combination of fear and excitement. The ground crew hustled around and then the basket rocked beneath her feet. She gulped and closed her eyes. The roar of the propane burners firing startled her into opening them again. The burners hadn't sounded this loud from across the field. The balloon slowly lifted off.

Andrea's pulse pounded. She wanted to inch closer to Clay, but she didn't dare move and rock the basket. Besides, Clay had already accused her—and rightly so—of trying to tempt him. She wouldn't give him the satisfaction of clinging to him. Clutching the four-foot high sides tighter, she watched her feet and concentrated on breathing normally.

"We'll fly at somewhere between five hundred and fifteen hundred feet off the ground, depending on the wind direction," Owen said.

High. Very, very high. Not good to know.

Clay covered her hand with one big warm palm and coward that she was, she soaked up his silent support. Countless minutes passed.

"Look," Clay spoke directly into her ear so that he could be heard over the noisy gas burner.

Andrea's racing heart stuttered. She forced herself to look over the edge of the basket and strangely, it didn't make her feel dizzy or sick. They'd cleared the tree line. The sun squatted like a big peach semicircle on the horizon, streaking the ocean with color. Dawn twinkled on the white, sandy beach. Fear loosened its stranglehold on her throat.

"See your house yet?" His breath stirred her hair and Clay's warmth spooned her back. Every molecule in her hummed with awareness of his proximity. When she shook her head he braced one arm on the side of the basket and reached around her with the other to point.

She swallowed the rush of moisture in her mouth and squeezed her thighs together in an effort to stop the tingle between them. How could she be getting turned on with a stranger standing within touching distance? She searched the direction Clay indicated until she found her robin's egg-blue cottage. Five years ago she'd bought an older home. It had taken years to totally renovate it from the garage at ground level to the widow's walk on the third floor. "Yes."

A radio transmission from the ground crew gave wind speeds and directions, but Andrea barely paid attention to the pilot's reply as she gazed in wonder at Wilmington and the southern North Carolina coastline blossoming beneath her. And then Owen turned off the burner and the silence overwhelmed her.

"It's beautiful." She loosened her grip, flexed her cramped fingers and looked over her shoulder at Clay. His warm, minty breath swept her cheek and his big body cradled hers. She stomped hard on the memories trying to crowd forward.

She turned and that left them kissing-close in the cramped basket. Clay looked totally relaxed. "You've done this before."

"Rod, my former boss, is into balloon racing. I've crewed for him a few times. There's nothing like the silence and the sensation of drifting on an air current."

Andrea blinked in surprise. This was a side of Clay she hadn't seen before. When they'd dated he'd been something of a control freak—not in a bad way as in wanting to control her. He just wanted things the way he wanted them. Precise. Logical. Orderly. He'd always been a black-and-white guy. Shades of gray hadn't been part of his color palette. What had caused the change?

"I would never have imagined you riding in a basket and letting the wind blow you wherever it dared."

His gaze locked with hers. "People change, Andrea. And you have more control over direction up here than you'd expect. Air currents at different levels travel in different directions. You choose your path."

Conscious of Owen standing just inches away, she nodded. Clay had changed and so had she. She'd gone from naive and trusting to sophisticated and guarded. She no longer believed in fairy tales and white knights, and while she wanted a happily ever after, she was more than willing to create that for herself instead of relying on a man to provide it.

That was what this bachelor auction deal was about. Choosing her path… Taking control, pointing her life in the right direction and going full speed ahead, and she would succeed no matter what the cost.

"Can you come in for a minute?" Andrea asked when Clay turned into her driveway.

"Sure." He'd barely seen her house in the predawn light when he'd picked her up. Like most beachfront homes hers had been built on pilings to keep it above the waterline in the event of a hurricane. The parking area beneath it had been enclosed. A three story windowed octagonal tower stood sentry on the left front corner. Soaring arched windows fronted the opposite side. The panes sparkled in the noonday sun. Clay followed Andrea up the curving stairs to her front door.

"Come in and have a seat. Can I get you something to drink?" She led him from the entry to the spacious living room overlooking the dunes and beach below.

"No. I'm good."

"Excuse me a minute." She jogged up the staircase, leaving Clay standing by the window with his hands fisted in his pockets and regret squeezing his chest. Sand-colored tile covered her floor and cool blue ocean colors dominated the upholstery. The glass-topped tables looked as if they'd been formed from driftwood. Splashes of orange, peach and yellow brightened the space, reminiscent of the beach at sunrise.

This was the dream house Andrea had described during those nights on his sloop, the house they'd planned to share.

She returned moments later, approached him and extended her hand. "I think it's time I returned this. I'm sorry I didn't send it sooner, but I didn't have your Florida mailing address."

Curious, Clay held out his hand. She opened her fingers and something small and light dropped into his palm. A tiny diamond winked in the sunlight streaming through the wall of windows. Surprise sucker punched the breath right out of him. His promise ring. The one he'd given her the night they'd graduated from high school—the night they'd made love for the first time and promised to spend the rest of their lives together.

The ring symbolized a broken promise and everything he'd lost. Because two people had lied. And because he hadn't had the guts to stay and see if he was made of stronger stuff than his father.

Even if he could have thought of an appropriate response, he probably couldn't have forced the words past the knot in his throat. He closed his fingers around the cool metal and swallowed.

"We need to put the past behind us, Clay." Andrea's eyes darkened with pain—pain he'd inflicted.

"Yeah. But you can keep this."

She put her hands behind her back. "I don't want it. I don't want to remember anymore."

He didn't want to remember either. But he couldn't forget.

Six

"I don't get in a race car unless I have a good chance of winning the race," Haynes called out as Clay passed the *Checkered Flag 3* early Thursday morning.

Grudgingly, Clay halted on the dock. Haynes's crew had left the day after they'd arrived, but the driver had remained behind like a splinter being shoved a little deeper beneath Clay's fingernail with each passing day.

"I study the other cars and the other drivers, and I gotta admit, Dean, you're giving me a run for my money that I didn't see coming."

Clay clenched his teeth. The man was a customer, so no matter how badly Clay wanted to tell him to go to hell and take his boat with him, he'd keep it polite. "There is no competition."

"Junior, you don't believe that any more than I do."

Three days had passed since the hot air balloon ride.

Three days of Andrea lunching on Haynes's boat and going out with him each evening. Three days of the promise ring burning a hole in Clay's pocket.

The man's presence had gnawed at Clay this past week until he had to face one indisputable fact. This wasn't a case of sour grapes—him not wanting Andrea, but not wanting anyone else to have her either. He was jealous. *Jealous.* He wanted Andrea for himself and after seeing her home—the home they could have shared—he realized the roots of his feelings ran deeper than he'd expected. He might even still love her.

"Think whatever you want, Haynes. Your motorcycle housing should be installed by this afternoon. You'll be free to go." He resumed walking toward his boat, his refuge.

"My money says I'll get her into the sack before you do, Dean."

Clay's muscles locked. Everything in him urged him to board the yacht and chase a few teeth down the jackass's throat with his fist, but Clay walked on, savoring one small victory.

Andrea hadn't slept with Toby Haynes. And Clay would do whatever he must to keep it that way.

The tingle was gone from Toby's kisses, Andrea fumed. And it was Clay's fault.

How could she think about a future with Toby—or any man for that matter—when her past with Clay kept slapping her in the face? Every touch and glance reminded her how good it had been between them before it ended. But her memories had been skewed by youth and blind love, hadn't they? He wouldn't pack the same punch now. Would he? Of course not.

She turned her head and looked at Clay across the front

seat of his rental car. He looked Miami-debonair in his pale sand-colored linen suit. He'd left the top two buttons of a shirt in the same shade of cobalt-blue as his eyes unbuttoned.

"For someone who wanted to buy his way out of these dates a few days ago you seem eager to get through them all."

Clay turned into the parking lot and turned off the engine. "Aren't you enjoying yourself?"

"Yes." So much, unfortunately, she'd neglected her agenda. Tonight she'd get it back on track. Come hell or high water, she would eradicate Clayton Dean from her thoughts. "But we don't have to rush to get through them."

"You'd rather I stayed on board and played solitaire every night while you're out with Haynes?"

She hadn't been out with Toby *every* night, but she didn't mind if Clay thought so. "No. You could visit your parents. Your father asks about you every day. You've been home thirteen days, Clay, and you haven't even called him."

Clay's expression hardened. He shoved open his door and rounded the car to help her out. The heat of his palm on hers addled her. She tried to pull free, but Clay wouldn't let go. Short of making a scene by struggling she was stuck walking so close beside him down the cobblestone sidewalk that their legs swished against their joined hands. Sparks traveled upward from each impact. Not good. Not good at all.

They passed the Renegade Bar and Grill owned by the bachelor Juliana had bought. For a moment Andrea considered dropping in to see if her friend and the rebel were together, but decided against it. Juliana had to work this out for herself, but Andrea sincerely hoped the biker would show her uptight friend a little of the excitement she'd been missing before it was too late.

A white flower-bedecked carriage, the kind used in

fairy-tale weddings, waited at the end of the block. Unlike the sleepy carriage horses Andrea usually encountered in tourist spots, the glossy white gelding in the harness looked alert and eager to go. The driver tipped his top hat. "Evenin', Ms. Montgomery, Mr. Dean. Climb aboard."

Andrea climbed into the carriage and stopped. A single peach rose lay on the seat. That particular shade—the color of sunrise—had always been her favorite. Had Clay bought the rose? Or was it part of the carriage ride package and the color choice coincidental? And what about the champagne bucket on the opposite bench? Clay's doing? Or had his mother arranged that, too? She preferred to credit Patricia because Andrea didn't want Clay doing nice things for her.

She lifted the flower and settled on the leather seat facing the horse. Clay sat beside her—too close for comfort. He stretched his arm behind her. She hugged her wrap closer, but the open weave of the crocheted fabric didn't protect her from his touch against her bare back. Clearly, the sexy halter dress had been a mistake.

The driver snagged the champagne bottle, popped the cork without spilling a drop and filled two flutes. He handed one to each of them and then stepped aboard and clucked to the horse. The sudden movement threw Andrea against Clay's arm. She quickly sat forward again.

Clay touched his glass to hers. "To the past and the future."

The carriage, flower and toast, combined with the clip-clop of the horse's hooves, tugged Andrea's heart like a riptide. She couldn't—*wouldn't*—be swept under Clay's spell again.

What better way to spoil the romantic mood than to find out why he dumped her? It took a second glass of champagne and fifty minutes of silent pep talk for Andrea to work up her courage. Even then, she couldn't force the words out until they rounded a corner and the carriage depot came into view.

"What did I do to make you leave?" she blurted with scant minutes left in their ride.

Clay whipped his head to face her and his eyes narrowed. "Nothing."

"Come on, Clay, we both know better than that."

Shutters slammed in his eyes. "Andrea, it wasn't you."

Was he lying? He had to be. "Then what?"

"Let it go."

"I can't." She wouldn't tell him about all the guys who had dumped her since he left. Her pride couldn't take it and she didn't want his pity. "If you'd messed up or had another one of your arguments with your father, then I would have heard about it. Joseph is known for verbally letting off steam."

Clay, with his back and shoulders stiffer than she'd ever seen them, looked away. "He never said anything?"

"Not one word. Which is why I know I was the cause."

The hand not holding his champagne flute fisted and a nerve beside his mouth twitched. "Dammit, you weren't."

"Then tell me who or what was. I didn't even know you'd returned from New Orleans that day until the receptionist stopped me on my way out to ask why you'd cut your visit short." Andrea twisted toward him on the bench seat. "Clay, why would you walk right past my office without bothering to say hello or goodbye when we hadn't seen each other in months?"

His jaw locked into rigid lines, but he didn't look at her. "I can't explain."

She'd had no idea this conversation would hurt so much or that once she worked up the nerve to ask her questions he'd refuse to answer them. "You just woke up that morning and decided to start over somewhere else?"

His gaze met hers and Andrea gasped at the agony in his eyes. Agony and secrets. Whatever the reason he'd left her it must be too horrible to share.

What was wrong with her? Did she lack some essentially feminine component?

"Andrea, it wasn't you. If you never believe another word I say, believe that."

She wanted to believe him. Really she did. But she had years of disastrous relationships and Joseph's silence as evidence that Clay was lying. "You used to trust me, Clay."

A disgusted sound erupted from his throat. He stared at the driver's back. "I used to trust myself."

His barely audible words staggered her. He'd found someone else. He'd moved on and left her stuck in the past.

The pain in Andrea's eyes gutted Clay. She'd been reticent since the carriage ride despite several attempts on his part to initiate conversation.

He followed her into her home. A single light glowed on an end table in her great room. She shed the white crochet stole she'd worn over her black-and-white halter-necked sundress and draped it over a chair.

The back of her dress left her bare to the waist. She wasn't wearing a bra and no tan lines marred her honey-toned skin. The front of her dress resembled a bathing suit with its gathered fabric cupping her breasts like a plump, mouthwatering offering. Knowing a single knot at her nape was all that kept him from cupping the soft swells had kept Clay at half-mast throughout the evening.

Andrea closed the blinds, blocking out the inky darkness of the ocean at night and the lights of a shrimp boat offshore. She faced him, knotted her fingers and bit her lip. "Was she better in bed than me?"

Shock stalled his heart. "What?"

"You said you used to trust yourself. That means you must have met someone in New Orleans. Someone who tempted you and turned you on more than I did. Someone who offered you more than what we had."

"Where in the hell did you get that crazy idea? There wasn't another woman, Andrea."

"Of course there was. Otherwise you would never have walked away from Dean Yachts. I know how much the company meant to you. But you're not the type to rub another woman in my face, and Joseph wouldn't have fired me or asked me to leave. So you left. You didn't have to do that, Clay. I could have taken it if you'd told me the truth."

How could she possibly believe he could love another woman more than he'd loved her? Clay crossed the room, clasped her upper arms. Her soft skin seared him. Knowing he shouldn't, but unable to help himself, he caressed her from her shoulders to her wrists and back.

"You're wrong. Dead wrong. What we had was good. Damned good. But it wasn't enough for me to forget—" For him to forget his father's infidelity or the fear that he was his father's son. He couldn't explain without saying something that would hurt her more. "It wasn't enough for me to stay."

She flinched. "Obviously."

She tried to pull free, but Clay held fast. He couldn't find the words to convince her that the problem hadn't been her, so he used only the weapon he did have, the passion simmering between them, and he started with the one thing he'd wanted to do since picking her up three hours ago. Hell, what he'd wanted every single day since she'd bought him two weeks ago. He kissed her.

Her lips remained unresponsive beneath his through the

first kiss. By the second she'd softened, and by the fourth she'd arched into him, wound her hands around his waist and welcomed his tongue in her mouth. The press of her soft flesh against him squeezed the air from his lungs. Gasping, reeling, he lifted his head.

Arousal flushed her skin and quickened her breath. The pulse at the base of her throat fluttered wildly. He pulled first one then the other chopstick-type things from her hair and the golden strands cascaded over the backs of his hands like cool silk. He dropped the hair sticks onto a nearby table.

His heart slammed into his ribs and his pulse nearly deafened him. How could the hunger be stronger now than it had been when he'd been head over heels in love with her? But it was. It swelled in him until he wanted to forget finesse and foreplay. He wanted to toss her back on the sofa and ravage her like a pirate storming a ship. He wanted to touch her, taste her and lose himself inside her until they were both too weak to move.

He stroked her lush bottom lip with his thumb and then dragged his hands from her shoulders down her satiny back to her waist and back again. She shivered against him and sighed a sweet breath against his skin. Desire expanded her pupils and darkened her eyes. Her high heels brought her forehead level with his chin. All he had to do was lean in to nuzzle her temple and pull her scent into his lungs. And then he had to kiss her again and again.

Common sense warned Clay to slow down and consider the consequences of his actions, but he couldn't. Years of denying himself what—who—he really wanted pulsed in his veins. He cupped Andrea's breasts and teased her beaded nipples, savoring her whimpers of pleasure. He traced the top of her dress, his fingertip meandering a drunken trail between cool fabric and warm smooth skin.

And then he discovered the zip at the back of her waist and eased it down. His hands dipped beneath the fabric to find silky panties and even softer skin. He cupped her buttocks and pulled her hips flush against his.

Andrea's breasts rubbed against him as she panted for breath. Her nails dug into his waist and then she tugged his shirttail free. Her touch on his back nearly brought him to his knees.

This wasn't about Haynes or his damned challenge. This was about making love to a woman Clay had never forgotten. If his feelings for Andrea hadn't diminished after eight years' absence, then maybe they never would. Maybe he hadn't inherited his father's weakness. Without a doubt she deserved better than him, but he knew for damned sure he had more staying power than Toby Haynes.

Her teeth nipped his neck and Clay shuddered. If he made love with Andrea tonight, he couldn't walk away from her again. What would it take to persuade her to give him a second chance? And if he succeeded would she be willing to pay the price? They couldn't live here and couldn't run Dean together the way they'd once planned. He'd have to convince her to come with him to Florida without telling her why they couldn't stay in North Carolina.

That might be his hardest job yet.

Revisiting the past was always a mistake. Tonight Andrea was counting on the fact that nothing was ever as grand through the eyes of maturity as the rose-colored memories of youth portrayed it, and if going to bed with Clay was the only way to prove that time had exaggerated his magic, then so be it.

Holly's warning slithered into her subconscious. Was she trying too hard to justify a bad decision? Was this a mistake?

No. Clay was like a hangover Andrea couldn't seem to shake, and the men at Dean swore the only cure for a hangover was the hair of the dog that bit you.

She linked her fingers through his and led him toward the stairs.

He halted at the bottom. "Andrea, are you sure?"

Sure that she wanted to be over him? Absolutely.

Sure that this was the way to go about it. Not so much. But nothing she'd tried in the past eight years had banished him, so what choice did she have other than to play this last card? "We have to do this if we're going to put the past behind us."

A frown puckered his brow. "Have to?"

"Have to." She released his hand and pushed his suit coat over his shoulders. Pulling it from his arms, she hung it on the newel post, and then moving quickly before she talked herself out of this, she released the buttons of his shirt. Once his shirt hung open, she stroked her fingers down the center of his chest, over his zipper and the rigid erection beneath it.

His breath whistled through clenched teeth. He caught her hand and dragged it upward. The dark line of hair bisecting his belly tickled her palm and then his hard, tiny nipple bumped beneath her fingertips. She could feel his heart pounding and then he lifted her hand and kissed her knuckles, her wrist, the inside of her elbow.

Dizzy with need, Andrea dragged in a much needed breath and backed up the stairs, leading Clay to her cathedral-ceilinged sanctuary. Moonlight streamed through the tall windows, illuminating her bed. She'd never shared her room with another man.

Not even Toby.

Toby. Her future. Maybe. Toby, who'd been amazingly

understanding about her preoccupation with work—meaning her temporary boss—and with her refusal to become intimate. Although his patience seemed to be wearing thin these last few days.

And then Clay's hands stroked from her waist to her underarms and back again. His thumbs swept beneath the bodice of her dress to brush the sides of her breasts and then beneath them. Thoughts of Toby evaporated.

Andrea's nipples tightened until they ached. She wanted—no needed—Clay to touch her. "Please."

"Please what?" he rumbled huskily against her neck. "This?" His thumbnails scraped over her nipples. "Or this?" He rolled the taut tips between his fingers.

"B-both." She bit her lip on a moan. He caressed her breasts and nuzzled her neck until her knees weakened.

When he removed his hands she opened her mouth to protest, but he captured her face in his palms and caught her words with his mouth. The passionate kiss dug deep, excavating memories and emotions she'd thought long since buried.

No, no, no. Sex with Clay wasn't supposed to be this good.

But it was. Desire smoldered in her belly, scattering embers of heat in all directions. She shifted restlessly, trying to stop the tingle between her legs, but the movement only exacerbated the situation because her wiggling brushed her breasts against his chest.

There was nothing familiar about the hot, supple skin of Clay's waist and back. Muscles she didn't recall undulated beneath her fingertips. His chest was the same. *Different.* But his taste... That she remembered.

He caressed her with a surety now, a single-minded determination to drive her absolutely witless that she didn't think she could have forgotten. Even if she'd tried.

His fingers tangled in her hair and then teased her nape. He released her and stepped back, putting scant inches between them. Cool air swept her hot skin. She forced her heavy lids open and realized he'd untied her halter dress. It fluttered to the floor, dragging over her sensitized skin like a caress to land beside the shirt he'd discarded.

When she stepped into his arms again the heat of his bare skin fused to hers. Breast to chest. Belly to groin. She struggled to recall her agenda.

Look for flaws. What is he doing wrong?

Nothing, absolutely nothing.

Look harder.

She reached for his waistband, released his belt and the hook of his pants and then glided the zipper down. His slacks and boxers slid over his hips and down his thighs with almost no effort, and then she caught her breath. The length and breadth of him hadn't been a rose-colored memory embellished by time and distance. The few lovers she'd had since Clay had not measured up. Damn. It.

Her fingers curled around him, stroking burning hot flesh and coaxing a slick droplet from the tip.

Clay groaned, caught her hand, stilling her. "Condom."

The enormity of what she was about to do hit her and she hesitated. Either sleeping with Clay was the right thing to do or it was very, *very* wrong. Did she dare risk it? She had to. The rest of her life was at stake. She couldn't continue living in limbo.

"Top drawer. Right bedside table." The reasons she'd bought the condoms nicked her pleasurable haze, but she blocked it.

He kicked his shoes and clothing aside, and she stepped out of her dress and heels. The sudden loss of height made her feel small and delicate. The top of her head barely reached his chin. Her mouth dried and her pulse pounded.

Cupping her buttocks, he bent his head and devoured her mouth and then shuffled her backward until the mattress bumped her legs. He released her only long enough to rip back her comforter. And then he stood and looked at her.

Moonlight flooded the room but shadowed his face. Did he like what he saw? She worked hard to stay in shape. She wanted him to drool. Wanted him to be sorry he'd walked away. Andrea thrust back her shoulders and his gaze immediately fell to her breasts. Clay had always been a breast man. Heaven knows he'd spent countless hours worshipping hers with his hands and mouth. The memory sent SOS flares through her bloodstream.

"Beautiful." He circled one areola with a fingertip, making her gulp back a whimper of need. And then his finger coasted down her breast bone, over her navel and along the elastic of her bikini panties. Her skin rippled in the wake of his touch and a shock of sensation whipped through her. His fingertip dipped behind satin, teased her curls, found her wetness and her pleasure point with accuracy that belied the passing of eight years. Unbearable tension blossomed at her core, making her shift restlessly. But he only allowed her a taste of what was to come before removing his hand. She nearly cried in frustration.

Clay knelt in front of her, rubbed his cheek against the triangle of fabric and inhaled deeply. She squeezed her eyes shut against the memories of him doing the same years ago. His palms opened over her hips and then stoked downward, easing her panties over her thighs, knees, ankles.

If this was a mistake, it was too late to turn back. Every cell in her body begged for more. She braced her hands on his shoulders and lifted one foot and then the other free of the fabric. From his kneeling position on the floor Clay rocked back and looked up at her. Her heart stuttered at the tension straining his face, but she couldn't see his eyes, and she needed to, needed to see if he was half as aroused as she.

Impatiently, she reached out and flicked on the bedside lamp. A peachy glow filled the room, but before she could read his expression Clay lowered his gaze to her tangled curls, lifted his hands to her hips and nudged her to sit on the bed. Andrea sat, because her legs were ready to collapse anyway. He outlined her dark blond triangle and then stroked her damp center with a lightly callused fingertip. She cried out at the potency of his touch. Need tightened inside her. His breath warmed her thigh and then he found her with his mouth. His passion-darkened gaze held hers as he tasted her, and every cell in her body turned traitor.

It wasn't supposed to be this good. Her fingers clutched the sheets and her head fell back. Her heels pressed the floor as she lifted her hips, silently begging him to give her the release she craved.

Clay's hands skated over her belly, her ribs and found her breasts. Trouble. Oh, was she ever in trouble. Good. Too good. Close. So close. She teetered on the edge of climax, her spine arching, her breath locking in her chest. And then he lifted his head. Frustrated and disappointed, Andrea sagged against the mattress with a muffled groan.

Clay yanked open the drawer, found and applied a condom. He rose over her, cupped her knees and pushed them upward, exposing her. His thick tip found her entrance and then he slid home in one deep, penetrating thrust. She banded her arms around him and tangled her legs with his, holding him close to savor the familiar sensations as they rushed over her.

She hadn't forgotten how well he filled her, how deep

he touched her or how perfectly they fit together. He withdrew only to plunge again and again, driving deeper, faster and harder with each thrust. Her body greedily lapped up every drop of sensation and hungered for more. Tension spiraled. Time hadn't exaggerated how swiftly he could propel her up and over the peak. Orgasm crashed over her with category five hurricane force. She muffled her scream against his shoulder and clutched his back, digging in her nails.

But Clay wasn't done. His mouth found her breast, sucking hard and drawing another gale of desire from deep within. His hips ground against hers, and then he kissed as if he couldn't get enough of her. She met him kiss for kiss. And then his face tightened and he groaned her name as he lunged once. Twice. The third time pulled Andrea into another vortex of passion she didn't have the strength to resist.

Clay braced himself on his elbows above her. Their bodies remained fused from ankle to chest, and the warmth of his breath steamed her sweat-dampened skin.

As Andrea struggled to regulate her own breathing a sobering thought crashed her back to dry land.

Clay hadn't disappointed her. Not even close.

Damn.

It.

Seven

A chime woke Clay from a sound sleep. He opened his eyes to unfamiliar terrain. Not his yacht. Andrea's bedroom. Last night flashed through his mind, and desire jolted his body like a lightning strike. For the first time in eight years he was right where he belonged. In Andrea's bed.

He turned his head and found her flushed face on the pillow beside him. Rolling to his side, he snuggled closer to her warm body, palmed her breast, nuzzled her soft hair and inhaled her scent. No perfume. Just pure woman with a hint of her coconut shampoo. A smile stretched his lips.

She stiffened and cursed, wiping his smile away as quickly as it had appeared. After one panicked look over her shoulder at him, she jerked upright in the tangled sheets and then flung back the covers and bolted into the bathroom chanting, *"Ohmygoshohmygoshohmygosh."*

He watched her adorable tush disappear around the

door with unease prickling the back of his neck. "Everything okay?"

She reemerged, hastily tying her robe and wearing a strained look on her face that didn't bode well for his morning appetite. "You're here. I overslept. No, everything is not okay."

The doorbell rang again—twice in rapid succession this time—and she winced. "Not good. Not good at all."

She hustled out of the room and down the stairs. He heard the front door open and then hushed voices carried up the stairwell.

Clay sat up, raked his hands through his hair and swung his legs to the floor. It was a good thing he and Andrea had taken a quick shower at 3:00 a.m. after making love that last time, because it didn't look like a leisurely shared bath would be on the agenda this morning. Even without the early morning visitor they had less than an hour to get to work.

Damn. He'd wanted to join her in that big whirlpool tub, lather every inch of her smooth skin and feel the jets swirling water around them while he buried himself deep inside her.

Next time.

He searched for his clothes and tugged them on. If he was lucky he could slip onto his yacht, shave and change without anyone at Dean noticing his wrinkled suit. He didn't want to make Andrea the object of gossip and speculation again, but sooner or later Dean employees would find out they were back together. From her less than lusty reaction this morning he gathered she needed a little time to get used to the idea.

He opened the cabinet over the bathroom sink, took a swig of her mouthwash and mulled over his last night's discovery. He'd fallen in love with Andrea again. Maybe he'd never stopped loving her. Whichever, he didn't intend to let her go this time. All he had to do was convince her to move to Miami.

He borrowed her hairbrush and then headed down the stairs. Who had the balls to drop in on her this early in the morning? It damned well better not be Haynes.

The voices—one too high-pitched to be the race car driver—led him through the den and into the kitchen. A boy with light brown hair sat on a barstool with his back to Clay. A backpack occupied the stool beside him. Who was the kid and why had he shown up at Andrea's door so early in the morning?

Andrea turned from the refrigerator, spotted Clay and froze midstep with an orange juice container clutched in her hand. Her mouth opened and closed, but no sound emerged and then her cheeks turned crimson. Her panicked gaze bounced from him to the kid and back again. The boy swiveled on the barstool.

Clay opened his mouth to say hello, but the words vanished. He stared at a picture of himself as a kid. Same sun-bleached hair, although the boy's was a few shades lighter. Same blue eyes. Same straight nose. His face and chin were a little rounder than Clay's had been. And that was Andrea's mouth, her full pouty lips.

"Clay, you should have waited upstairs," Andrea said.

He didn't even look at her. Couldn't pry his gaze off the boy. "What's your name, son?"

"Tim Montgomery. Who're you?"

Possibly your father. His lungs squeezed. "Clayton Dean."

The kid's eyes lit up. "Uncle Joseph's Clay?"

Uncle? "Yeah. How old are you, Tim?"

"Seven."

Clay's heart and lungs stalled. He'd fled Wilmington

eight years ago without once looking back to see what re-percussions he'd left in his wake. He'd left a big one.

He had a son.

Why hadn't Andrea told him? How could she have kept his child a secret? How could his mother? Patricia Dean had known how to reach him. The old anger and betrayal reared up inside him, but he tamped them down. He didn't want his son's first impression of his father to be that of a raving lunatic. But Clay was furious. More furious than he'd ever been in his life.

And he was scared. Damnation. He had a son and he knew nothing about kids.

Tim swiveled back and forth on the stool. "Andrea's taking me to work today 'cuz of school. Maybe I can work some with you, too?"

Andrea? He called his mother by her first name? He looked up to see a tender smile on Andrea's face. She filled the boy's glass and ruffled his hair. Tenderly. Lovingly. As a mother would.

Another wave of anger broadsided Clay. She'd denied him the opportunity to love his son. His jaw and fists clenched. He deliberately made himself relax one knotted muscle at a time. "It's June. Why aren't you on summer vacation?"

"Tim's in the year-round program," Andrea answered for the boy. "Today is take-your-child-to-work day, but since my mother is retired and my father is out of town on a weeklong business trip I volunteered to let Tim shadow me."

Her father and mother? "What do your parents have to do with this?"

Andrea put away the juice and then stared at him for several heartbeats. Confusion puckered her brow. "Tim is my brother."

Brother? Like hell. The kid was the perfect combination of Clay and Andrea. How could she deny her own child? Why had none of the gossipy workers at Dean told him Andrea had borne his son? Because they protected her. Because they remembered the way Clay had hurt her.

"Andrea, could I speak to you upstairs?" He barely managed to force the words out past the fury crushing his windpipe.

Wariness entered her eyes. She clutched her robe tighter. "Sure. I need to get ready anyway. Finish your cereal, Tim. I'll be right back and then we'll go."

Clay took another lingering look at his son, trying to absorb every detail, from the cowlick on the back of his head to the missing front top teeth, scraped knee and double-knotted sneakers. A lump rose in his throat. He'd missed so damned much.

He turned and gestured for Andrea to precede him and then followed her upstairs and into her bedroom. He closed and locked the door. "What in the hell do you mean, *your brother?* That boy's mine."

Shock slackened her features. "He is not."

"You're lying."

"Do I look like I've had a baby? You were certainly close enough last night *all three times* to see any stretch marks or scars." She sounded insulted, indignant.

If she'd had any signs of pregnancy, he'd been too busy making up for lost time and reeling from the discovery that he still loved her to notice. "He's mine," he repeated. "Why else would you look panicked when I saw him?"

"Because my little brother can't keep a secret. He'll blab to anyone who'll listen that you were here this morning and I wasn't dressed. I do not need that broadcast all over Dean."

What she said made sense, but it was still a lie. It had

to be. "He looks like me. How in the hell could you deny me my child?"

The confusion in her eyes turned into sympathy. She touched his arm. He yanked away, unwilling to let her dilute his anger with passion. "Clay, Tim couldn't possibly be yours. For one, I would know if I'd given birth. Two, he was born in February. The last time we slept together was New Year's Day before you graduated in May."

February. Was she lying? You couldn't fudge a birth date by six months. And then it hit him, knocking the strength from his legs and sucking the air from the room. He sank down on the rumpled bed and dropped his head into his hands. *February.*

He'd caught his father and Andrea's mother in May. He did the math and came up with nine months. Damnation. Tim wasn't his son. He was his half brother, a product of his father's adulterous affair with Andrea's mother. He had to be. Both of Andrea's parents were blondes, and the kid had brown hair. While Andrea's father had blue eyes they weren't *that* shade of blue—the blue Clay saw in the mirror each morning. And Clay… Clay was a chip off the old block. No wonder the boy looked like him.

"I can't believe you think so little of me that you'd believe I'd hide your child from you. Or that your mother or father would let me." She picked up a pillow and whacked him across the back with it. Anger, not embarrassment caused the redness in her cheeks. He could hear it in her clipped words, see it in her mast-straight posture, but most of all, he saw honesty in her eyes.

His heart rate slowly returned to normal, but his mind and stomach churned. He pinched the bridge of his nose. He wasn't a father. He was a brother. A half brother to Andrea's half brother. How damn twisted was that?

Did his father know? Did his mother? Did Andrea's father?

She crossed to the bedroom door, unlocked and opened it. "Please go, Clay. I have to get dressed. I'm running late and we have a delivery today. I have loads to do."

Once more her mother and his father had capsized Clay's world. Tim was a living, breathing reminder of his father's infidelity. And Clay couldn't tell Andrea. He rose. There was so much to say and none of it could be said. Last time he'd run. This time he couldn't. He wouldn't walk away from her again.

He wasn't his father. If he still loved Andrea after all these years apart, then he would love her until he took his last breath.

But this wasn't just about him and Andrea anymore. An innocent boy could be hurt. Clay had to find out who knew the truth about Tim's parentage. That meant he'd have to talk to Andrea's mother, and even though he'd rather swim through an alligator-infested swamp, he'd have to talk to his father.

He paused in the open door inches from Andrea, close enough to feel her heat and inhale her scent. Even his shocking discovery this morning wasn't enough to stop the rush of hunger through his veins. "We'll talk tonight."

He lifted a finger to brush her cheek and bent to kiss her, but she flinched out of reach. "There won't be a tonight, Clay. Last night was a mistake. Blame it on nostalgia or hormones or whatever you want. I won't sleep with you again. I have my future planned and it doesn't include you."

Her words hit him with a staggering blow, but he didn't go down. He had his work cut out for him. He would change her mind.

* * *

Considering the incredible night Clay'd had, this was turning into one lousy morning.

The first person he saw after passing through the Dean's gate was Toby Haynes. The race car driver sat on his yacht's back deck sipping from a mug, and while Clay would rather ignore him, courtesy demanded otherwise. "Morning, Haynes."

"Dean." The man's eyes traveled from Clay's unshaven face to his rumpled suit and back. "Wild night?"

As much as Clay would love to tell the jerk exactly where he'd been, what he'd been doing and who he'd been with, he wouldn't. "You're up earlier than usual."

"Waiting for Andrea. Thought we'd share coffee this morning. But she's late."

Clay hesitated. "She'll be here soon and she has Tim with her. It's take-your-kid-to-work day."

"Not surprising. She's nuts about that kid. And you know this how?"

Clay ignored the question. He wouldn't lie. "Enjoy your coffee."

He walked toward *The Expatriate.* Toby's laugh made him turn back.

"Son of a bitch. Never let it be said I'm a poor sport." The race car driver lifted his mug in salute. "This round to you, pal. But don't get cocky. I'll be back to give you another run for your money. Andrea's worth the effort and I mean to have her."

Clay's competitive hackles rose. Not for the first time he wanted to knock the jackass over the rails. "By all means, come back when you're ready to order *Checkered Flag 4,* but Andrea and I won't be here."

"Why's that?"

"My business is in Miami."

A smartass smile played about Haynes lips. "If you think she's going to leave this and go with you, then I gave you too much credit in the smarts department. Andrea won't leave Wilmington or Dean."

"You're wrong."

"Want to put money on that wager, junior? Because this looks like a sure-fired winner for me."

Pressure built in Andrea's chest until she was ready to scream.

At the rate she was going she'd never be ready for the delivery celebration in time. She took a deep breath, tried to concentrate on the multitude of details yet to be handled and tried even harder to block out the Technicolor flashbacks of last night that kept blindsiding her. It wasn't easy when each movement, each shift of her suit over her supersensitized breasts made her remember.

The sex had been incredible. Otherwise, she would have booted Clay out of her bed after the first time. But after a long drought of delicious partner-induced orgasms she'd greedily indulged in every morsel of satiation Clay had offered.

Peter, bless him, had come after Tim, claiming he needed "help" that only the seven-year-old could provide. Andrea hoped the pleas she'd made on the drive to work would keep Tim's lips zipped about Clay being at her house so early in the morning.

Clay, damn him, had been in and out of her office half a dozen times in the three hours since she'd arrived. Add in a surprise visit from Octavia Jenkins and the last thing Andrea's frayed nerves needed was to hear a helicopter approaching.

Please, please, please don't let the new clients arrive early. Their yacht isn't even at the dock yet.

She hadn't had time for a cup of coffee and caffeine withdrawal was kicking in. She pressed a hand to her throbbing head. A tap on her door drew her gaze away from the window and an entirely new tension squeezed her temples.

Guilt swamped her. "Toby. Good morning."

"Morning, angel." He crossed the room, but stopped on the opposite side of her desk. No good morning kiss. And that worried her less than it should have. She wasn't the type who could kiss one man and then kiss another only hours later. "I'm heading out today."

She blinked in surprise. "But you have another week left in your vacation."

He shrugged. "I'm gonna head back to the track. I shouldn't have taken time off midseason anyway. My relief driver is struggling. The boys will take the yacht."

That was not relief coursing through her veins. Was it? Damn Clayton Dean for confusing her. "I'm sorry to see you go."

"I'll be back. Count on it." He winked.

Behind her, the *thwump, thwump* of the helicopter setting down shook the windows and rattled her aching head.

"That's my ride and my crew. Don't go giving your heart to somebody else while I'm gone, Andi." He tugged on the brim of his racing cap, pivoted and left. Without a kiss goodbye.

Andrea sank into her desk chair, propped her elbows on her desk and dropped her head in her hands. Her future had just walked out the door while her past resided at the end of the dock like a blot on her personal landscape. She'd counted on this week clearing the decks. Instead, the past several days had made her more confused and depressed than ever before.

She didn't love Clay. And she never would again.

But she seriously doubted she'd ever be able to love anyone else.

Damn. It. Damn. Him.

No sooner did the helicopter lift off than Clay walked in again carrying a mug of coffee. She was almost grouchy enough to wrestle it from him.

"What now?" She winced at her bitchy tone.

Clay took one look at her face and passed her the mug. "Careful. It's a New Orleans brew. Stronger than you're used to."

How did he know she needed a caffeine fix? And then she mentally smacked her forehead. They'd shared enough mornings on his old sailboat for him to know she couldn't start her day without coffee. She wrapped her fingers around the warm mug, inhaled and then took a sip. Bliss. "Thank you."

"You're welcome. Mind if I show Tim *The Expatriate?*"

Mind? She could kiss him. No. She couldn't. No more of that. "I'm sure he'd like that."

"I can keep him occupied until the party if it would help."

Why did he have to be nice? She didn't want him to be nice. "That would be great."

She wanted him to be the selfish bastard who'd broken her heart. The selfish *forgettable* bastard who'd broken her heart. Because then it wouldn't be hard to let him go. Again.

On the back deck of the Dean sales office Andrea glanced furtively around and then dialed her friend's number on her cell phone. The new owners were due within the hour and her nerves were shot. She took a moment while the caterer set up the champagne lunch to escape.

"Rainbow Glass. This is Holly."

"I messed up," Andrea whispered.

"Oh, Andrea. What did you do?"

"I slept with Clay." Silence greeted her confession. "Go ahead and say it."

"I'm too good of a friend to say I told you so. So why did you? Sleep with him, I mean."

Andrea raked a hand through her hair. "My reasoning seemed logical at the time. Sex was supposed to be anti-climactic, disappointing."

"And it wasn't."

"No. It was good. Better than I remembered." Her skin flushed. "Damn. It."

"Do you still love him?"

"No. For heaven's sake, *no*. Are you crazy?" She darted a glance toward the dock. "How could I love a man who'd hurt me that way? I'd have to be an idiot to go back for more."

"What about Toby?"

"He's gone. He left an hour ago, and even though he said he'd be back, I get the feeling he won't. He didn't even kiss me goodbye." Andrea bowed her head. "Holly, I've done it again. I've killed another promising relationship."

"I know you don't want to hear this, but good riddance. Juliana and I both think Toby was only after the conquest. Once you'd slept with him we think he would have sailed off into the sunset."

Were her friends right? No, they couldn't be. They hadn't spent hours with Toby, hadn't witnessed his gallantry or the way he treated her like she was the most important thing in his life…next to racing.

"I think you're wrong, Holly. This thing with Toby has been going on for years." And her heart could learn to pitter-ter at his touch with a little practice. She was sure of it.

"You mean he's been toying with you—like a cat does a mouse—for years."

The blast of an air horn startled her and she almost dropped the phone. Andrea spun toward the dock as the crew maneuvered the newest yacht into the slip recently vacated by the *Checkered Flag 3* to ready it for the delivery celebration. Tim manned the horn on the fly bridge. She could see his elated grin from a hundred yards away. She waved and then Clay climbed to the top deck and stood beside him.

Andrea's stomach dropped like an anchor. Tim did resemble Clay. The startling thought stole her breath. But how could that be? It couldn't. It was simply coincidence.

"Holly, can we do lunch really soon? I want to hear about you and Eric. I still think you cheated by buying Juliana's brother instead of that gorgeous firefighter, but Octavia could be right. Eric might be the right guy for you. Opposites attract and all that."

"Shut up, Andrea Montgomery. That article was inexcusable, and you can bet I'm going to strangle Octavia for writing such dribble. Eric is a friend. That's it. No matter how good-looking he is."

"So you admit he's handsome." Holly sputtered, but a signal from the receptionist caught Andrea's eye. "Look, Holly, I have to go—the new owners are here and I have Tim today. Crazy day."

"After a crazy night. Andrea, stay out of trouble and out of Clay's bed until you figure out where you want this to go. He's not staying. Remember that."

How could she forget? He'd leave her just like last time. And she still didn't know why she was so dumpable.

Elaine Montgomery looked stylish and far younger than her age with her blond hair upswept and her pantsuit skimming her slender curves. Heads had turned as she crossed the restaurant, heading for the table where Andrea waited. But as usual, Andrea realized, her mother didn't notice the attention. Andrea could only hope she'd look as good when she reached her fifties.

"Aren't Holly and Juliana joining us tonight?" her mother asked as she slid into the booth across from Andrea at the trendy new restaurant on Market Street.

"No. They're busy with their bachelors. What about Patricia?"

"She's stuck to Joseph like a stamp on an envelope. She hasn't left his side since the stroke except for the day of the bachelor auction, and then she hired a nurse. I had hoped Clay would stay with Joseph some and give Patricia a break. I don't think she would agree to leave Joseph with anyone else again. Heaven knows, your father and I as well as most of the Caliber Club members have offered."

The diamond eternity band Andrea's father had given her mother for their thirtieth anniversary several years back sparkled in the overhead light and Andrea felt a twinge. At the rate she was going she'd never get a wedding ring let alone another piece of jewelry to celebrate reaching a marriage milestone.

"I'm working on Clay, but he still refuses to speak to his father and he won't tell me why. So it's just the two of us again this week." Andrea welcomed the waiter's arrival because it gave her time to organize her thoughts. After he took their drink and appetizer orders and left she noticed the tension around her mother's mouth. "Is everything okay?"

Her mother's smile looked forced. "Of course. And before I forget, Timmy had a wonderful time today. Thank you for taking him. You know how much he loves spending time at Dean. I left him chattering nonstop to your father about his day and Clay. I think he has a new hero."

Andrea concealed her wince and hoped Tim would keep her secret.

"How is working with Clay going?"

Her mother had no idea what a loaded question she'd asked. "He handles the details of Dean like a pro. Joseph will be pleased."

"But?"

Where should she start? With her mistake last night or with Clay's odd accusation? Normally, she and her mother were as close as sisters, but Andrea wasn't ready to share her blunder because she didn't understand it. In her head she knew sleeping with Clay had been a stupid and stupendous mistake—one she couldn't repeat no matter how loudly her body clamored for his. But each time he'd touched her today—and he'd done so often during the delivery celebration—her hormones had thrown a party worthy of Mardi Gras. She'd felt as drunk and dizzy as if she'd partied on Bourbon Street all night even though she hadn't touched a drop of the champagne they'd served.

In a way, she had partied all night. Her skin flushed at the scorching memory of how many times and how noisily she'd partied. She grabbed her ice water and sipped. "Who in our family has dark hair?"

Her mother looked up abruptly. "Why?"

"Because Clay thought Tim was his son." She snorted in disgust. "As if I'd keep something like that from him. But he said Tim looked like him. And I guess Tim does a little. I think it's mostly because of the hair and the eye color. Daddy has blue eyes, but I couldn't figure out where the hair came from."

The waiter arrived with their drinks and salads and then took their entrée orders and departed.

The ice in her mother's glass tinkled as she lifted her

Tom Collins to her lips. "Your great-grandfather, my grandfather, had dark hair, and I'm sure there are other relatives on your father's side, but at the moment I can't recall who."

"Then I guess Tim's a throwback." Andrea speared a cherry tomato.

"Yes." Her mother lowered her drink and reached for her salad fork. "Tim said that was Clay's car I saw in your driveway this morning when I dropped him off."

Andrea's appetite vanished. She toyed with her salad. So much for secrets. "Yes."

"Do you think it's wise to become involved with him again?"

"I'm not."

"Andrea, his car had dew and sea spray all over it and the hood was cool. He hadn't arrived recently."

Andrea cringed. "I just want to get over him, Mom. I thought sleeping with him would do the trick."

Her mother covered her hand. "Oh honey, that never works."

"How would you know? You met Daddy in high school and you've been together ever since. Why can't I find a perfect love like that?"

Elaine lowered her gaze, but not before Andrea caught a glimpse of deep sadness. "Love is never perfect and I did have a life before your father, you know."

Andrea blinked in surprise. "I thought Daddy was your first love."

"Harrison was my first lover and he's the love of my life. I count my blessings every day for him."

First lover?

Her mother and father had been high school sweethearts. They'd married right after college—just like Andrea and Clay had planned. When had her mother had time to take another lover? If she and Andrea's father had broken up at some point and then reunited, they'd never mentioned it. Had her mother's word choice been a slip of the tongue?

As close as she and her mother were, Andrea was certain she didn't want to hear about her mother's intimate life. So she let the subject drop, but that didn't stop the questions from tumbling through her brain.

Eight

Clay paused in his morning run long enough to buy a Saturday newspaper from the local convenience store. After checking the score for the Marlins game he turned to Octavia Jenkins's second installment.

Clayton Dean seems eager to monopolize Andrea Montgomery. Sources say the former lovers have completed four of their seven dates in only two weeks. Is that because Clay fears the sexy contender vying for Andrea's affections or because the old ashes aren't as cold as they claim? This reporter has learned that it's not only Andrea's sunsets Clay's after. The couple has shared a few sunrises, too.

Damnation. It's a wonder Andrea hadn't hammered on his door before dawn again this morning to chew him out.

She'd like this installment even less than the last one. Clay folded the paper and jogged back toward Dean.

His pulse kicked up a notch and it had nothing to do with his pace. He wanted to see Andrea again. The sooner, the better. They had three dates left, and he would use them to convince her to come with him to Miami. No matter what the car jockey said, Clay knew he would succeed. Failure wasn't an option.

Clay turned up Dean's mile-long driveway. He'd been stymied in learning more about Tim's parentage. Last night he'd invited his mother to dinner to quiz her to see what she knew. She'd countered by issuing an open invitation for him to eat with her and his father. Clay had refused. He wasn't ready to face Joseph Dean yet.

That left Elaine Montgomery. Clay intended to corner her as soon as possible and he had the perfect excuse. Tim had left his hand-held video game on Clay's yacht yesterday.

Two hours later Clay rang the Montgomery's bell. Elaine opened the door. Her eyes, the same caramel-brown as Andrea's, widened with surprise and a hint of fear.

"Clayton. How n-nice to see you." She lied politely, but not well.

"May I come in?" Surprisingly his voice didn't reflect his inner turmoil even though betrayal burned like acid in his throat.

Her reluctance couldn't have been clearer. Last night had been girls' night. Had Andrea told her mother about Clay's reaction to meeting Tim?

"I have Tim's video game." He dangled the canvas carrying case from his fingertips.

"Tim and his father have gone fishing. I'll give it to him when he returns. Thank you for bringing it." She reached for the bag. Clay moved it out of reach.

"His father?" This time the sarcasm seeped out.

Elaine's face paled and tensed. "Come in."

She led him to the living room. It looked the same as it had eight years ago. He and Andrea had made out on that couch too many times to count. "May I get you a drink?"

He couldn't pretend this was a social call. "Does my father know?"

"Know what?" she asked, feigning ignorance, but the woman would never make it as an actress. The way she twisted her wedding ring around on her finger and the slight quiver of her lips gave her agitation away.

"Don't play games with me, Elaine. Tim is my father's son."

She drew herself up, lifting her chin in the same way Andrea did when preparing for battle. "You are mistaken. Harrison is Tim's father in every way. His name is on the birth certificate."

"That may make him responsible in the eyes of the law, but that boy carries Dean DNA."

She opened her mouth, but Clay cut her off. "Don't waste my time with lies. I want to know who knows, and if my father does, then why didn't the bastard do something?"

"And what would you have him do? Force me to have an abortion? Divorce your mother, the woman he loved more than life, and destroy two families on the possibility that Tim *might* be his?" She hurled the words in a burst of temper.

What right did *she* have to be angry? She'd ruined his life not the other way around, and if he were as selfish as his father, he'd consider returning the favor. But taking Elaine Montgomery and Joseph Dean down meant taking Clay's mother and Andrea down, too. "If he loved her, he wouldn't have cheated on her."

"We're not perfect, Clay. None of us. And that includes

you." Shoulders drooping, she sank into a chair. "We all make mistakes." She wrung her hands, looked away and then met his gaze. "Don't blame your father for this. It was my fault."

"It takes two."

"You don't understand."

"Then explain it to me. How could you betray your husband and your best friend? And how long was the affair going on?"

She hesitated long enough that Clay thought she wouldn't answer, and then she lifted her head and met his gaze. "It was only that one time. Your father and I both regretted our lapse immediately. We knew how much our selfishness could cost us and the ones we loved, and we vowed it would never happen again. And it didn't. When Joseph realized you'd left and you weren't coming back it hit him hard. And I felt doubly guilty for having been a part of what drove you away. What you saw that day should never have happened."

"If you loved your husband so much, why risk an affair?"

Sadness and regret filled her eyes. "Because a long time ago I was in love with your father, and then he met my best friend. From that moment on Joseph didn't have eyes for anyone else. Patricia became his world."

Surprised, Clay lowered himself to the sofa. In all the stories his parents and Andrea's had told about being high school sweethearts, they'd never shared this part. "You married another man."

"Yes, and I love Harrison, but it wasn't the same as the love I felt for your father. You never forget your first love. That's why you'll never forget Andrea or she you.

"When I hit forty I started wondering what I'd missed by marrying so young and not seeing the world, and in not becoming your father's lover when I had the chance. Stupid of me to yearn for the what-could-have-beens when I had everything. A husband who pampered me. A beautiful, talented daughter. A million-dollar home. And I..." She paused, closed her eyes and took a deep breath. When she lifted her lids he saw strength and resignation on her face. "I seduced your father, Clay. Not deliberately or maliciously. But the result was the same.

"I was forty-seven years old. It never occurred to me that I could get pregnant. Harrison and I had tried for years after Andrea was born to conceive another baby. We'd always wanted a large family. As soon as the doctor told me I was expecting I was overjoyed. It wasn't until later that the doubts and the fears crept in, and I realized I didn't know who the father was. And it could have been either of them."

He flinched. Too much information.

"I had a difficult pregnancy from the very beginning, so I quit my job. And honestly, I was relieved because then I didn't have to face Joseph or the shame on his face every day. Because of my age I was more concerned with whether or not my baby would be healthy than I was with whose DNA he carried. Either way, Tim was a blessing. He was born as bald as a cue ball. His baby hair came in the same dark blond Andrea's is now and his eyes were blue like my husband's. It wasn't until Tim approached his third birthday that both darkened. We do have some dark-haired relatives."

He didn't want to feel sympathy for her, dammit, but the fire of hatred he'd fanned for eight years cooled a little.

"Does my father know?" he repeated.

"He's never asked and I've never volunteered the information. The same goes for Harrison and your mother."

"How could she look at Tim and not see me?"

"Tim takes after me in many ways, and Clay, love is a powerful thing. It can make you overlook what you don't want to know. In fact, none of us truly knows who Tim's father is. We've had no reason to have DNA testing done. And the blood types are inconclusive."

"Does your husband know you cheated? Does Andrea?"

"No. It was over. It couldn't be changed. And it wasn't going to happen again. Telling them would only upset them and cause pain. So I didn't. Harrison adores Tim. I would never do anything to drive them apart."

Her confession confirmed that Clay couldn't tell Andrea why he'd left without hurting her or Tim. So where did he go from here? "I love your daughter."

"Do you?" She sounded skeptical.

"I won't leave Wilmington without her this time."

"If you'd loved her enough, you wouldn't have left her the last time."

Clay sucked a sharp breath at the unexpected attack.

"And if you truly loved your father, you'd forgive him for not being perfect, and you'd quit punishing your mother for something that wasn't her fault."

He'd be damned if he'd be lectured to by the woman who'd almost wrecked his family and still could if this news got out. He stood and stalked toward the door. His hand closed around the knob.

Elaine pressed a hand to the door, holding it closed. "You were the most important thing in Patricia's life, Clay. You can hate me if you want to, but she didn't deserve what you did to her. And neither did Andrea."

Clay glared at Elaine Montgomery, jerked the door open and left.

The truth stung.

Andrea used to love Mondays, the promise of a new week, the excitement of what she could accomplish in the next five days and interacting with the employees as they gave shape to customers' dreams with fiberglass and wood. But her love of Mondays had turned to dread since Clay's return.

These days she stayed as tense as a flag pole, waiting for Clay to walk in or worse, summon her to his "office" as he had this morning.

She gathered the necessary files and made her way down the dock in her rubber-soled Docksides and a pantsuit. No more sexy shoes or short skirts. Mission accomplished. She'd made Clay want her. But her goal had backfired because the reverse was also true. He'd made her want him.

The sun beat down, promising another scorching June day with suffocating humidity, but today, thanks to Olivia's article, Andrea's temper rivaled the weather. She boarded Clay's yacht and spotted him at his desk/galley table and then knocked on his door with more force than necessary.

He lifted his gaze from the documents in front of him and the impact of those blue-blue eyes hit her like too many caramel apple martinis on an empty stomach. *Toughen up, girl.*

With a jerk of his chin he motioned for her to enter. The door glided open easily beneath Andrea's fingers, and the air-conditioning swept over her, cooling her skin but doing nothing for her temper or the warmth settling in the pit of her stomach.

"Sit down. Did you bring the prospective client list?"

She deposited the files in front of him and slid into the seat farthest away from him. Unfortunately, that gave her an unobstructed view of the companionway leading to his stateroom.

Tim had chattered incessantly about the cool gadgets on Clay's boat, piquing Andrea's curiosity, but she didn't dare ask for a tour. If she went below decks and heard the slap of the waves on the hull, her resolution to keep her distance would probably crumble under the weight of her memories of his tongue stroking her mouth, his hands on her breasts and his hips grinding against hers.

Blinking away her distraction she focused on her notes. "The Langfords are visiting tomorrow to order a seventy-foot sport-fishing craft. The Richardsons will be here on Friday. They're not sure exactly what model they want, but they can afford almost anything we build. I've also included two new appointments that aren't on your calendar. All four couples have been financially prescreened."

He glanced at the paperwork and then pushed it aside. "I've made reservations at Devil's Shoals Steakhouse for us tomorrow evening."

Alarm skittered over her. Devil's Shoals was the most romantic and exclusive restaurant in the area. "No."

"What do you mean, 'no'?"

"I'm getting pitying looks from the staff because of Octavia's story. I will not go out with you and have them think I'm stupid enough to fall for you again. From here on you'll see me at work and nowhere else."

A line formed between Clay's eyebrows. "We have three dates left."

"As the one who purchased your auction package I have the right to cancel the dates. I'm exercising that option."

"What about the publicity?"

"Forget it. I'd rather not have it than have this…bilge."

He rolled his pen between his fingers—the same way he'd rolled her nipples. Heat filled her cheeks and her panties, and her traitorous nipples tightened. Andrea looked away and ended up staring at the corner of his bed. Damn. It. Why couldn't the sex have been lousy? And why couldn't she forget how *un*lousy it had been?

"My mother invited me to dinner," Clay said quietly.

"That's wonderful."

"I won't go alone."

Every muscle in Andrea's body tensed with dread. *Don't ask. Oh please, don't ask.* "I'm sure you can find a date."

"I'll go only if you'll come with me."

"Don't be ridiculous. Your parents want to see you not me."

"Fine. I'll send my regrets."

Andrea fisted her hands beneath the table. She'd promised to do whatever it took to get Clay and Joseph together. Going to dinner would accomplish that goal. If she was lucky, this goal wouldn't backfire on her the way the other one had. Sleeping with Clay had been a rotten idea. How had she talked herself into it?

"All right. But this isn't a date. I'll meet you there."

"No deal. I'd show up and you wouldn't. I'll pick you up at six and we'll go together or not at all."

He had her and he knew it. She wanted to scream. Instead, she forced herself to nod. "I'll be ready."

A whirlpool of emotion twisted in Clay's belly. Anger. Resentment. Betrayal. Guilt.

His hand shook as he extracted the keys from the ignition and stared at the large Colonial house where he'd grown up. A smarter man would put the car in gear and drive away. Even with Andrea looking beautiful and sexy in a flirty yellow sundress by his side this wouldn't be a pleasant night.

"Clay?"

He blinked. Andrea stood beside his car in the semicircular driveway. He hadn't even heard her get out of the vehicle.

The front door opened and his mother stepped out onto the deeply shaded, two-storied, columned porch. As a kid

Clay had shimmied up those columns like a monkey does a tree much to his mother's dismay and his father's amusement. But it had been years since he'd felt so carefree.

No backing out now. He'd come this far. And dammit, he wasn't a coward. Years of anger, acrimony and accusations bubbled like lava inside him waiting for release. Tonight he'd confront his cheating father with the facts the minute he got him alone.

He shoved open his door, joined Andrea and walked beside her up the wide brick walk.

"Hello, dear." His mother greeted Andrea, kissing her cheek, and then she turned to Clay. Her arms banded around his middle and she hugged him tight enough to squeeze the breath from his lungs. When she drew back tears glistened in her eyes. "Welcome home."

Guilt burned him like battery acid as Elaine's words replayed in his head. *She didn't deserve what you did to her.* "Mom, it's good to see you."

What else could he say? It *wasn't* good to be home. Clay examined her carefully made-up face, noticing the lines of strain he'd been too angry to see the day of the auction. His mother looked older, tired, nervous.

"Come in, come in. I've been cooking all day. I made all of your favorites, Clay." Clay followed the women inside.

"Where was Dora when you invaded her kitchen?" The cook and housekeeper had been with them since Clay's teens.

"She played cards with your father and the occupational therapist while I cooked, and tonight is her bingo night."

Occupational therapist? Clay looked to Andrea for explanation. Sadness tinged her smile. "Is poker still the only way to get Joseph to do his exercises?"

Exercises? His mother had said his father's stroke had been a mild one, that he'd be as good as new in no time.

She turned toward the living room which surprised Clay. His family had always preferred the sunken den at the back of the house with its view of the Intracoastal Waterway to the rarely used formal room on the street side. The living room furniture had been pushed apart and the coffee table removed.

And then he saw his father and Clay's world stopped. The slam of his heartbeat in his ears drowned out his mother and Andrea's conversation. The stooped man in the chair bore little resemblance to the robust man Clay had cursed for eight years.

A lopsided smile lifted the right corner of his father's lips, drawing attention to the drooping muscles on the left side of Joseph Dean's face. He tried to stand and immediately Clay's mother rushed to his side to help him because he couldn't do it alone.

He couldn't do it alone.

Andrea, in the guise of giving Joseph a hug, pulled him to his feet and steadied him. "Hi, handsome. I hear you're beating the pants off the therapist again."

"I'm trying. Have to get even for what she puts me through." His father's voice sounded weak, more like the voice on the phone than the forceful tone Clay remembered. It was only then that Clay noticed the metal walker to the right of his wingback chair.

Andrea stepped aside, but Clay noticed she didn't go far. One of her hands rested on his father's waist, tightening when Joseph lifted his right hand and wobbled on his feet.

Clay's shoes seemed leaded. With great effort he forced his feet forward to accept his father's handshake.

"Good to have you home, son." His father's voice broke and tears filled his eyes.

"Dad." Shocked by his father's weakness, Clay looked away. Why hadn't anyone warned him? And then Clay realized Andrea had tried and he'd refused to listen. In the past two weeks he'd cut her off each time she'd mentioned his father.

And then it hit him why they were in the living room. His father probably couldn't manage the three stairs down into the den.

"Why don't you two sit down and catch up," his mother said, gesturing for Clay to take the wing chair beside his father's. She and Andrea tried to help Joseph sit, but he irritably waved them away and slowly, awkwardly worked himself back into his seat.

His mother touched Andrea's arm. "Honey, I could use your help in the kitchen."

Clay's gaze met Andrea's as she passed. He found sympathy and understanding in her eyes. Her hand caught and squeezed his and then she let go before more than a spark could ignite.

The door between the dining room and the kitchen swung closed behind the women. Alone at last. Clay fisted his hands and took a deep breath and faced his father. This was it. The opportunity he'd been waiting for to tell his father exactly what he thought of him. To tell him about Tim.

But Clay couldn't do it. He couldn't verbally strike the weakened man in front of him.

But he would. Later. When his father was stronger Clay would tell him how badly he'd screwed up his life. For now he'd stick to a relatively safe topic—business.

Concerned by Clay's silence, Andrea turned on her front mat after unlocking her door. He hadn't spoken since leaving his parents' home. "Clay, are you all right?"

Her porch light illuminated the strain in his strong face,

the down-turned corners of his lips and the crease between his eyebrows. "I didn't know he was this bad."

Where was the satisfaction she'd expected to feel? She'd wanted Clay to be shocked, wanted him to feel guilty for not rushing to Joseph's bedside immediately following the stroke and for refusing to see his father since coming home. And yes, as petty as it now seemed, she'd wanted to scare Clay into acknowledging that he could have lost his father without healing the breach between them.

But instead of gloating over the success of the evening, she felt Clay's pain, remembered the shock of seeing a man she revered brought to his knees—literally and figuratively. She'd had five weeks to come to terms with the changes in Joseph Dean. Clay had had mere hours.

"His prognosis is good."

"He can barely walk. His left hand is practically useless."

"The physical challenges will improve with continued therapy. He's already made great strides since it happened."

He swallowed visibly and raked a hand through his hair, ruffling it the way she had Thursday night. Her fingers curled around the memory and her pulse stuttered. Damn. It.

"He was worse than this?"

She nodded. "The doctors say he'll make most of his recovery in the first few months and then continue at a slower rate for the rest of the first year afterward."

He blinked and straightened, but his eyes still looked shell-shocked. "Thanks for going with me."

"You're welcome. Are you going back to your yacht now?"

He shook his head. "I need...to think. I'm going to drive around awhile."

As distracted as he seemed, driving wouldn't be safe. The road was loaded with summer tourists who had no idea where they were going. It took full concentration to avoid an accident.

Without a doubt Clay needed comfort, but Andrea feared that if she invited him inside she'd give in to her overzealous hormones and comfort him in bed. Despite changing the sheets and spraying perfume on her mattress, her bedroom still smelled of Clay. He inhabited her dreams every night as surely as if he lay beside her in the bed. Instead of erasing the memories, sleeping with him had apparently refreshed and reinforced them. She couldn't stop thinking about him, about his touch, the warmth of his breath on her skin or the surge of him deep inside her.

A shiver started in the pit of her stomach and worked its way to her extremities in the form of goose bumps. She rubbed her hands along her upper arms. "Want to take a walk on the beach?"

He shoved his hands in his pockets, looked at his car and down the street and then his gaze returned to hers. "Sure."

She led him through the den, pausing to shed her sandals and drop her purse in a chair while he kicked off his leather deck shoes and rolled the legs of his khaki pants to midcalf. He followed her out the back door and down the steep steps to the beach. The moon whitewashed the water and the day's warmth lingered in the sand sifting between her toes. A balmy breeze blew off the ocean, rippling the hem of her sundress against her knees and tossing her hair.

They walked a half mile in silence, side by side like the old days, but back then they would have been wound around each other or at the very least, holding hands. Andrea realized Clay was no longer beside her. He'd had stopped a few yards down the beach while she was lost in the past. She backtracked and stood beside him.

He exhaled and shoved his hands in his pockets. "Tell me what happened."

She'd expected him to ask during dinner. Instead he'd turned into the man who'd cohosted the delivery celebration with her Friday afternoon. He'd been polite, but distant, keeping the conversation impersonal and treating his mother and father more like clients than family.

"Joseph had an embolic stroke. That's caused by a clot that travels through the bloodstream and lodges in the brain, cutting off blood flow and damaging the affected cells."

"Who found him?"

A weight settled on her chest. Andrea stared at the undulating water. "I did. We were due to go on a sea trial after lunch. Joseph was late, but I thought he might still be on the phone with one of our more demanding clients, so I kept working. When I finally went looking for him, I found him on his hands and knees in the middle of his office." Guilt closed her throat. "If I'd gone sooner—"

Clay caught her arm and pulled her around to face him and then he released her just as quickly, but the heat of his touch remained imprinted on her skin. "There's no way you can blame yourself for this."

"Joseph is never late for anything. I should have checked on him earlier."

"Why didn't he call for help?"

"He couldn't. His speech was affected. Luckily, the medicines they gave him at the hospital reversed that. You probably noticed he's still a little slow to find the words, but he does find them, and his thought processes are clear."

"He's very…emotional."

Clay's embarrassment over his father's tears had been obvious. "Another side effect of the stroke is having trouble controlling emotions. That, too, should improve."

Clay tipped his head back and swiped his face with his hand. "He won't be able to return to work in two months."

"The doctors said he might be, but in a reduced capacity. He needs your help, Clay, for as long as you can give it."

The moon blanched all color from his face. "Dammit, I have my own company to manage. I can't stay here."

"Could you relocate Seascape?" She wanted the words back the moment they left her mouth.

What are you saying? Do you want him to move back home?

No. Definitely not. She couldn't face him and the hunger she felt for him on a daily basis, because she could never trust him not to hurt her again. If he returned she'd have to leave Dean and leaving Dean would break her heart. She'd invested the love in the company that she couldn't find in her personal life. The staff was like an extended family.

He stalked toward the waterline, stopping only when an incoming wave lapped at his ankles. "I am returning to Miami. I can't…stay here."

Andrea dampened her dry lips. Her heart thudded heavily and her palms moistened. She loved Patricia and Joseph Dean almost as much as she did her own parents, and the Deans would be overjoyed if Clay returned to Wilmington and took his rightful place at Dean Yachts. She had to do everything in her power to make that happen.

Inhaling deeply, she braced herself to ask the question she'd known all along she would have to ask. "Would you stay if I resigned?"

Fists clenched, Clay rounded on her and splashed back in her direction, stopping only inches from her. "Dammit, Andrea, I told you you're not the reason I left."

She lifted her chin to meet his gaze. "But you won't

explain why you did, so until you level with me, Clay, I have to go with what the facts tell me. And the facts tell me I'm the reason you and your father aren't speaking."

His jaw muscles bunched. His brow creased and his lips compressed. For several seconds he held her gaze and she thought he might actually tell her what she desperately needed to know. She tensed in anticipation, in dread. *What is wrong with me? Why does every man I care about dump me?*

"I want to talk to his doctor."

She blinked at the abrupt change of subject and her lungs deflated. "I'm sure that can be arranged. Ask your mother to set it up. And while you're at it, you might want to consider offering to watch your father once in a while. Patricia has barely left his side since this began, and she needs a break before she collapses."

"I'll talk to her about hiring some help."

But he wouldn't offer to stay with his father. Andrea sighed. Her job was far from done.

Nine

Would you stay if I left?

Clay focused on Andrea's words as they retraced their path. Her question proved she was willing to leave North Carolina. Haynes was wrong.

He didn't want to think about watching his father sip from a straw because Joseph couldn't drink from a glass without dribbling down his shirt. Clay didn't want to think about his father's lasagna being served in child-sized bites because he couldn't manage a knife. Clay didn't want to think about what would happen to Dean when he returned to Miami.

He didn't want to think. Period.

What he wanted—*needed*—was a night of hot, sweaty sex to distract him from the ache in his chest dinner had left behind. Heartburn. That's all it was. The pain had nothing to do with the shock of seeing his father tonight and everything to do with the spicy meal—even if Italian food had never bothered him before.

He'd had a setback in his plans, but that didn't mean he couldn't keep moving forward in his quest to convince Andrea to go back to Florida with him.

On the concrete pad at the base of her steps Andrea turned on the spigot to rinse the sand from her feet. Clay eased his foot between hers underneath the gushing faucet. He brushed his toes over her ankle, around her heel and stroked the gritty sand away from her instep. He heard her breath catch and bit back a satisfied smile. Andrea had always loved a foot massage and he'd give her a good one. Upstairs. Preferably naked.

She gripped the banister and lifted a suspicious gaze to his. "What are you doing?"

He rested his hand beside hers on the wood, fingers parallel and touching hers. Only inches separated their bodies and an ocean breeze lifted strands of her hair to his cheek, snagging the silken threads in his evening beard. "Washing my feet. And yours."

He shifted his leg, dragging the inside of his thigh against hers, but stopping his knee short of her panties. The cool water rushing over his feet did nothing to cool his quickly rising libido.

Her lids lowered and she swallowed. "Don't, Clay."

"Don't what?"

The look she aimed at him said she was wise to his strategy. "Don't try to tempt me back into bed."

Guilty and totally unrepentant, Clay felt a smile twitch on his lips. "Is that what I'm doing?"

She backed up the bottom step, putting distance between them but raising her eyes level with his. "I know you're upset. Tonight must have been hard for you, but I'm not interested in a temporary fling."

He turned off the water and straightened. "Who said anything about temporary?"

"You did when you said you were leaving."

Cupping her jaw he looked deep into her eyes. "Come back to Miami with me."

Her eyes widened and her lips parted on a gasp. Before she could voice the objections he saw chasing across her expressive face, Clay covered her mouth with his. At the touch of her soft lips, desire, hot and instantaneous, flared in his blood. He climbed the step, crowding their bodies together on the narrow tread, and then banded his hand around her waist to pull her soft, warm curves closer.

She couldn't possibly miss his erection against her stomach. He wanted her. Bad. No other woman had ever been able to draw such an immediate response from him. If that wasn't love, then what was it?

Her palm flattened against his belly as if to push him away, but she didn't. Good thing. He'd have tumbled backward onto the concrete at the bottom of the steps. For safety's sake he shifted sideways and nudged her back against the railing which freed his hands to comb through her hair, down her spine and over her hips to tease the small of her back with his fingertips. He coaxed her mouth with his, twining his tongue with hers and nipping at her bottom lip until his head spun.

Andrea's nails scraped over his waist and a shiver shook him. He cupped her breast, flicking his thumbnail over the hardened tip. She moaned into his mouth and then tore her lips away from his and turned her head aside, granting him access to the pulse fluttering wildly at the base of her throat. She tasted good, smelled good, felt so damned good in his arms. How had he lived without her for eight years?

Her breasts shuddered against his chest and then her fingers tightened, pushing him away this time. "Stop."

"Stop what? This?" He caught her earlobe in his teeth and gently tugged a gasp from her. "Or this?" He rolled her nipple between his fingers.

"B-both." Arousal flushed her cheeks.

Clay lifted his head and lowered his hands to her waist. Her panted breaths and expanded pupils told him she wanted him as much as he wanted her. "Let me make you feel good, Andrea."

She stiffened and frowned. "Why? So you can hurt me again later?"

"I won't hurt you, babe. Trust me."

She wrenched from his arms and raced up the steps. At the top she turned to watch his slower ascent. "That's the problem, Clay. I don't trust you anymore and I never will again."

Whoa. Her words set him back.

She unlocked the back door and stepped inside, scooped up his shoes and then stabbed them against his chest. "Go."

He searched for a way to salvage the evening, a way to get his plans back on track. If he could get her into bed, he could remind her why they belonged together. He dragged a fingertip down her arm. "Andrea—"

She turned on her heel, crossed the den and yanked open the front door. "Get out, Clay."

All right, so maybe he was moving too fast for her. He had six weeks left to change her mind. He could afford to be patient. "I'll see you in the morning."

"Not if I see you first," he heard her grumble a split second before the door slammed.

Andrea made good on her threat by avoiding Clay for a day and a half. Those thirty-six hours dragged by like weeks, distracting him from his enjoyment of his temporary job.

As an independent naval architect he drew the plans for yachts and then the owners took them to the builder of their choice to have the craft built. More often than not Clay never saw the finished product. This week he'd worked on blueprints for two customers—not his original designs, but adaptations of Dean designs. If he stayed, he'd get to see the finished vessels launched and christened.

Don't go there. You're not staying. Which means you need to focus on Andrea.

Andrea's avoidance of him made his decision to seduce her into returning to Miami with him all but impossible. She'd quit coming in early to have her coffee on the deck, and every time he went looking for her he found her surrounded by Dean employees.

Today, he intended to put an end to her evasive tactics. He rapped on her open office door and the look of consternation on her face when she spotted him confirmed his theory that the minute she saw him head up the dock she made herself scarce. He'd been in the fiberglass building when she arrived this morning and therefore, she hadn't seen him coming.

He leaned against the jamb. "I'm taking Tim fishing this afternoon."

"Why?"

Because he wanted to get to know his little brother. "We have nothing scheduled, and from what Tim said the other day that kid loves to fish as much as I did at his age."

"But Tim's in school."

"Your mother's bringing him over after he gets out."

Andrea blinked in surprise. "My mother has approved this?"

Elaine didn't dare refuse given that Clay knew her secret. "Yes. You're welcome to join us."

She bit her lip. "But I—"

"Have an empty calendar this afternoon. I had Fran check." He ran his gaze over her sedate black pantsuit. If she thought dressing like a nun would make him forget what a few pieces of fabric concealed and how good they were together, then she was mistaken. Men loved mystery—at least this man did. Besides, the suit and the lacy top she wore beneath it were sexy in a subtle way.

"Eve also told me you keep sunscreen and a swimsuit here. Bring them."

Andrea shuffled the papers on her desk and then laid them aside. "Clay, this isn't a good idea. Perhaps another time—"

"Be on the dock by three or we'll leave without you." Clay turned on his heel and left before she could argue.

He would win her back. Failure wasn't an option. And he was counting on her protectiveness of her little brother to bring her to the dock.

Trapped.

Andrea sighed and tucked a stray lock of hair beneath her hat. How had she let herself be coerced into this? Because she hadn't wanted Tim to get any more attached to Clay than he'd already become. Clay would leave and Tim would be hurt. She ought to know.

Clay dropped anchor in a small inlet off Masonboro Island. There wasn't another soul in sight other than an occasional boat passing by in the waterway. Even though they were surrounded by wide open spaces, sharing the small skiff with the man who enticed her to throw caution into the winds was like being locked in a cell with temptation. She couldn't escape unless she trudged through the marshy water to the uninhabited barrier island and took her chances with the foxes and the alligator some claimed to have seen basking on the beach.

Clay's brief red trunks showed his tanned muscular legs, broad shoulders and six pack abs to advantage. Each time he passed by her seat in front of the center console he managed to brush his warm, hair-roughed skin against her and whip her hormones into frenzy. The man was hell on her nerves.

And Tim was in heaven. He hadn't stopped chattering since they'd left the dock. And Clay… Andrea shook her head. She never would have expected Clay to have the patience of a saint, but he answered each of Tim's questions—no matter how foolish or repetitive.

He'd be a good father.

Andrea winced at the stab of regret and focused on the shoreline. Eight years ago she'd thought he'd be the father of her children. But she'd been wrong. Painfully wrong.

Tim tilted his head and laughed at something Clay said, yanking Andrea's gaze back to the fishermen. Her heart skipped a beat at the similarities in their stance and then she shook her head. Damn Clay and his insane allegation that Tim was his son. Because of it she kept seeing similarities—gestures, the slant of Tim's smile, a teasing twinkle in her brother's eyes—between the males that she knew were a figment of her overactive imagination. Tim had probably picked those up from Joseph or copied them from Clay the other day. Her little brother had a budding case of hero worship.

What would hers and Clay's children have looked like? The question caught her by surprise and an old, familiar ache squeezed her chest. *Let it go. The past is the over and you're not going to let it repeat itself.*

"You're turning pink," Clay said, yanking her out of dangerous territory.

"I forgot to put on sunscreen." She reached into her bag and withdrew a tube. Clay plucked it from her hand.

"I can do it," she protested.

"You can't do your back. Turn around."

Not a good idea. Not good at all. But with Tim watching she could hardly refuse without sounding ungracious and rude and Clay knew it. What game was he playing? Reluctantly, Andrea turned. Clay sat behind her on the narrow bench. His thigh pressed against her bottom like sun-baked sand, only firmer. His big, slightly roughened hands descended on her shoulders, and the heat of his touch combined with the sun-warmed lotion stole her breath.

He massaged the upper portion of her back and then dragged languid fingertips down her spine. She shivered. Silently cursing her telling response, she crossed her arms over her tightening nipples. There was no way to hide her goose bumps. His palms glided over her ribs, her waist, the small of her back and then back up again. His fingertips brushed the sides of her breasts. Arousal swirled beneath her bikini bottom and made her breasts ache.

She kept her gaze fastened on Tim, trying to recall why she'd come today, but desire weighted her eyelids. Clay's hands dipped over her collarbone and she ached for him to go lower, to stroke her breasts, to tease her nipples with his lotion-slickened fingers.

She caught herself leaning against him, yanked her eyes open and bolted to her feet. Damn. It. She had absolutely no willpower where Clayton Dean was concerned. It wasn't fair that the one man she couldn't trust would have so much power over her. Why had no other man been able to reduce her to a puddle of need?

Come back to Miami with me, his voice echoed in her head. He didn't mean it. If he truly wanted her back, he'd tell her the truth. And until she knew the truth she couldn't risk the past coming back to bite her. Whatever had driven him away eight years ago still lurked like a shadow ready to enclose her in darkness again—darkness she very nearly hadn't escaped. If not for her friends, her job and later, her baby brother, she probably wouldn't have.

She snatched the sunscreen from his hand. "I can manage the front."

Clay's hot gaze glided from her face to her breasts, her waist and lower, and her double-crossing body responded as if he'd touched her. She wished she'd had a less revealing swimsuit in her drawer, but she'd bought the miniscule black bikini with Toby and the hot tub on his yacht in mind. Not that she'd ever had the chance to wear it. She'd had a feeling that being half-naked with Toby would lead to being totally naked, and that was a step she hadn't been ready to take.

"Sure you don't want help rubbing it in?"

The husky timber of Clay's voice brought a flood of moisture to her mouth and other areas she refused to ac-knowledge. "No."

"Let me know if you change your mind."

"I won't." But she wanted to. She wanted his hands to retrace the path his hot gaze had taken. Where was her common sense?

"I got a fish!" Tim squealed and Clay immediately left her side to help Tim reel in his catch.

Weak-kneed with relief, Andrea sank back onto the bench. She was in trouble. Big, big trouble. And she had absolutely no idea how she'd survive another six weeks without jumping Clayton Dean.

"I need a favor."

Andrea looked up from the most recent customer satis-faction survey to see Juliana Alden, one of her best friends and partners in the auction scheme standing in her doorway. Juliana stopped by Dean often enough that Eve knew to let her back without buzzing Andrea.

"Sure. Name it."

Juliana entered and closed the door. "Rex is refusing to see me. I know this sounds adolescent, but it's really, *really* important. I need you to go to his bar and see if he's there. I'll wait outside. If you see him you can call me on my cell and I'll come in before he can hide again."

Her uptight bank auditor friend had bought the former Nashville bad boy hoping he could teach her how to have fun, but from the pallor and stress on Juliana's face it didn't look like fun had been on the program. "Sounds easy enough. Are you all right? You're pale."

"Yes. No. I don't know." Andrea's brows rose. The indecisiveness did not sound like Juliana. "I can't talk about it yet. But soon. I promise. Okay?"

Andrea nodded. She, Juliana and Holly had always met once a week either for girls' night out or for lunch, but their auction packages had wreaked havoc on their usual get-togethers. They couldn't even celebrate Holly's thirtieth birthday. But now more than ever Andrea needed the girl talk.

"What about you and Clay?" Juliana asked as if reading Andrea's mind.

If anyone could make her see reason, then Juliana—the queen of logic and level-headedness—could, but Andrea didn't know where to start.

"I slept with him. It was…incredible. I can't get him out of my head. I just *want* him. But I can't risk loving him again because all he talks about is going back to Miami. He even asked me to go with him." The words gushed from her mouth without pause for breath.

Juliana's dark eyebrows lifted. "Would you be willing to go with him?"

"Of course not. Everything that's important to me—my friends, my family, my job—are here in Wilmington. And there's no way I'd leave Joseph at a time like this. Besides, Clay doesn't mean it. He just wants to get me back into bed."

"And you want that too."

"Well…yes, but he's *leaving*," she repeated. "Again."

Juliana sank into the chair in front of Andrea's desk. "Aren't you the one who talked me into buying a bachelor we all knew was totally wrong for me just for the chance to have great sex?"

Andrea winced. "Yes, but that's because you're about to get engaged to a cold fish. You've never had great sex, so you need to see what you're missing before you give up on it."

"And aren't you the one who said women should be more like men and learn to keep love and sex separate?" She held up a hand halting Andrea's protest. "Aren't you the one who said, 'Why should we limit ourselves to self-induced orgasms when there are capable men out there'? Aren't you the one who sings the Tina Turner song, 'What's Love Got to Do With It?' in the shower?"

Andrea cringed and considered crawling under her desk. "That might have been me, but—"

Juliana snorted. "No might about it. Practice what you preach, Andrea, and sleep with Clay while you have the chance. You know he's leaving, so you won't fall in love with him again. It'll just be sex—great sex. But short-term, like a sex vacation."

Andrea frowned. "Who are you and what did you do with my conservative friend? And is sex with Rex really that incredible?"

Color rushed to Juliana's pale cheeks. "Your conservative friend is starting to loosen up a little, and yes, making love with Rex is better than any fantasy I could have imagined. I'll never be happy with vanilla sex again." She rose, looking embarrassed by her confession. "So...can you get away now? I really have to talk to Rex."

"I'll get my keys."

"Andrea, will you think about what I said?"

A sex vacation with Clay. How could she think about anything else?

"What's going on?" Andrea called from her open doorway.

Clay stopped in the hall, parking the hand truck loaded with boxes outside his father's office. "I'm moving my office inside."

Andrea's lips parted and her breasts, covered in a lavender lingerie-style top, rose. Her legs shifted beneath a deeper purple slim-fitting, knee-length skirt and once again she wore seriously sexy high heels. "Oh."

As much as he hated working in the room where his world had crashed, Clay thought he stood a better chance of winning Andrea over to his way of thinking from twenty feet away than from a hundred and twenty yards.

She tucked a long golden lock of hair behind her ear. "Can I speak with you when you have a minute?"

He studied her serious expression and watched her nibble her lush bottom lip—something he'd like to do. "I have time now."

He followed her into her office. She closed the door behind him, walked toward her desk and reached for the matching suit jacket hanging from her chair and then she stopped and turned without donning the concealing jacket.

He silently thanked her for giving him the opportunity

to savor her curves in the satiny fabric. Was she wearing a bra under that top? He'd love to find out firsthand, *hand* being the operative word.

"I changed my mind about dinner."

Surprise yanked his gaze back to hers. "Why?"

Her fingers curled by her side. "Do I have to have a reason?"

"Andrea, you always have a reason, usually an entire list of reasons."

Her cheeks flushed. "Yes. Well. I also start what I finish. I bought your auction package and I'll see it through."

She didn't sound overjoyed, but he'd take what he could get and make it work to his advantage. "I'll set up the date."

"But I have a request. I'd like to keep what happens between us from the staff and Octavia Jenkins. My personal business is just that. Personal."

A needle of regret jabbed him. If he'd learned anything in the three weeks he'd been back it was that his dumping Andrea had been common knowledge at Dean. And in the past few weeks he'd interrupted enough conversations to know that the staff was taking bets on whether or not he and Andrea would end up together or he'd leave her again. This time she wouldn't have to endure the embarrassing gossip because he'd take her with him when he left Wilmington. Although after seeing his father he wasn't sure when that would be.

"Agreed. We'll keep it as private as possible. When would you like to go out?"

"The sooner the better."

Her response jacked his libido up a notch. Now that's more like it. "Tonight?"

"Okay." She nibbled her lip again and then slid into her desk chair. She fussed with the pens on her desk, aligning them in a perfect row, and then she met his gaze. "And Clay? Pack an overnight bag."

Shock dropped his jaw and sent his blood rushing south. He didn't know what game Andrea was playing, but he wasn't about to argue since she'd just made his seduction plan a hell of a lot easier. "Yes, ma'am."

He'd give her a night she would never forget, and he would earn her trust.

A sex vacation. Ohmygosh.

This had to be the craziest thing Andrea had ever done. Sex for sex's sake. Sure, she believed a woman had the right to go to bed with a man without expecting wedding bells, but she'd never tried meaningless sex or even wanted to. Until now.

She pressed a hand over her frantically beating heart, took a bracing breath and opened her front door. Clay stood on the doormat with a duffel bag hanging from his shoulder and a large shopping bag in each hand. He looked edible with his white dress shirt unbuttoned at the neck and black pants hugging his hips. And he smelled edible too, crisp and clean with a hint of lime.

"What's all that?" She nodded at the shopping bags.

"Our date."

"Aren't we were going to Devil's Shoals?"

"I thought we'd stay in tonight." He smiled, a smile filled with seductive promise.

Her pulse stuttered. "Then I hope you have dinner in one of those bags because my cupboards are nearly bare."

"I have dinner…and a whole lot more." His gaze meandered over her loosely upswept hair, her black silk tank dress, her legs and her heels and then back again. "Beautiful and very desirable, Ms. Montgomery."

Her knees weakened at the appreciation in his eyes and the sexy growl of his voice. She suddenly felt hot and damp all over, but that was probably caused by the warm rush of humid air from outside. "C-come in."

She closed the door behind him and tried to catch her breath. "The kitchen's this way. Let me help you unpack."

"No."

She stopped. "Excuse me?"

Clay dropped his duffel bag at the foot of the stairs and then carried the bags to the kitchen and set them on the counter. He returned to her side, cupped her shoulders and steered her toward the sofa. "You relax. I'll handle everything."

A warm puff of breath was her only warning before his lips brushed her bare nape. She tried to face him, but he held fast. "Sit. I'll bring you a glass of wine."

Andrea sat. The sofa faced her fireplace, leaving her back to the kitchen and Clay. Fabric rustled behind her and then something dropped over her eyes. A blindfold? "Wait a minute."

She reached for the black material and then Clay's breath teased her ear. "Trust me."

Swallowing her nervousness, she lowered her hands. Tonight was all about pleasure—physical pleasure. And if Clay wanted to play sex games, then she could be woman enough to play along. The fabric tightened as he knotted it at the back of her head. "This is crazy."

"Trust me," he repeated just before his tongue traced the shell of her ear. She shivered.

That was the problem. She didn't trust him. Not completely. Sure, she knew he wouldn't hurt her physically, but she didn't trust him with her heart. But her heart wasn't at stake tonight, was it? She'd locked it securely away.

No love. Just sex.

And if she repeated it often enough it would be true.

His lips grazed the side of her neck, choking off her ability to reason. She sucked in a sharp breath. His fingertips skated over her shoulders, her collarbone and then dipped to outline the deep V-neck of her dress. Her nipples tightened in anticipation, but he withdrew his hands leaving her with an unsatisfied ache in her belly.

His footsteps retreated to the kitchen. Cabinets opened and closed and then a bag rustled, followed by the pop of a wine cork and a splash of liquid. Footsteps approached and her pulse accelerated. The cool rim of a glass touched her lips. She sipped cautiously. Cool chardonnay—a good one— filled her mouth. Clay lifted her hand and wrapped it around the wineglass stem and then returned to the kitchen.

Andrea drank her wine and listened to the unfamiliar sounds of a man in her kitchen. She heard him extract a plate from the cabinet, but not the clank of pots or pans. He must have brought takeout.

She felt as much as heard Clay join her. And then the sofa dipped as he settled beside her. She inhaled, but before she could identify the tantalizing aromas something warm, moist and slick nudged her bottom lip. She slipped her tongue out to taste. Butter?

"Open."

She obeyed and Clay fed her a morsel. It took only seconds to identify her favorite food, lobster with drawn butter. The next bite revealed Chinese green beans, tangy with soy sauce and ginger, and then a spoonful of wild rice with raisins and almonds. He'd remembered her favorites. She tried to harden her heart, but there was no denying the warmth spreading through her.

With bite after bite Clay satisfied one appetite but

roused another with the brush of his fingers on her lips, his thigh against hers and the occasional press of his arm against her breasts when he reached across her for the wineglass he'd set on the end table.

When he left her again her tensed muscles eased. She sagged into the cushion and squeezed her thighs together. How could she get turned on by this blatant seduction routine? It was ridiculous how easily he'd manipulated her. If she had any sense at all, she'd rip off this blindfold and—

The cushion sank again and adrenaline raced through her. Something cold touched her lips. She opened her mouth. French vanilla ice cream, rich, creamy and delicious, melted on her tongue. But after a few spoonfuls she held up her hand. "I can't eat any more."

Glass clinked as he set the dish down on her coffee table, and then his lips covered hers, a breathtakingly hot contrast to the cold dessert. Her nails dug into her palms as she fought the urge to wind her arms around him. Arousal blurred the edge of reason.

Just sex. Don't get emotional.

All too soon he lifted his head. "I'll be right back."

She heard him moving around the kitchen. A bag rustled and then he climbed the stairs. What was he doing? And why didn't it bother her to have him roaming through her house? She'd never given any other man free rein of her home.

Trust him. And she realized she did in a way she'd never trusted any of the other men she'd thought she might eventually marry.

What felt like ages later but was probably no more than five minutes, she heard him jog down the stairs. Clay approached, captured her hands and pulled her to her feet. He led her across the room and then slipped an arm around her waist. "Careful on the steps."

He guided her upstairs. The sound of water running greeted her when they reached the landing and grew louder as she entered her bedroom. In her bathroom, she inhaled a mixture of flowers and spices. Not her perfume or her bubble bath. Clay released her and turned off the water and then his palms glided over her shoulders, down her arms and back again. He pulled her back flush against his front and his erection pushed against her spine. She gasped and need twisted deep inside her.

"Andrea, if you didn't intend for us to end up in bed together tonight, now's the time to tell me," he whispered against the sensitive skin beneath her ear.

Ohmygosh. She struggled to find her voice. "I did. I do."

His fingers tightened on her arms. "You won't regret it."

That's where he was wrong. She was certain she would and probably already did. This whole blindfold/feeding thing was slipping past the defenses she'd worked so hard to erect.

He found the zip at the back of her dress and pulled downward. Cool air swept her spine. She trembled. Clay eased the straps over her shoulders and then held her hand as she stepped out of the dress.

She squared her shoulders. What did he think of her black push-up bra and sheer, miniscule panties? His groan answered her unspoken question. "You're even more beautiful now than you were eight years ago."

The reminder gave her a twinge of discomfort, but she tamped it down. She wanted to see his face, to look into his eyes and see if he meant the compliment, but she kept her fingers clenched by her side. The blindfold frustrated her.

You're a thirty-year-old woman. Play the game.

His shirt brushed against her thigh as he knelt, and then his fingers curled around her ankle. He removed one shoe and then the other. His fingers skimmed up her legs and briefly cradled her bottom before he flattened his palms over her belly and urged her against his hardness. She rocked her hips to torment him and was rewarded by a low groan. His cheek pressed hers and she imagined him watching the two of them in the wide mirror behind her vanity.

When she'd renovated the house she'd taken a smaller bedroom and converted it into a hedonistic master bath complete with a glass shower stall which they'd used last time he was here and a tub big enough for two on a raised platform. Would Clay join her in the tub?

Desire swirled through her with dizzying force. She'd never been so turned on in her life. She wanted to grab his hand and tuck it between her legs. Instead, she gulped, squeezed her knees together and squirmed.

The cadence of Clay's breathing deepened, quickened. His short nails scraped lightly above the elastic of her panties and then beneath the band of her bra. Her stomach muscles contracted involuntarily and she sucked a sharp breath. With a flick of his fingers the front clasp of her bra gave way. Hot palms cupped her, kneaded her. Her lips parted in an effort to pull air into her lungs. She sagged against Clay, savoring the light abrasion of his hands against her flesh and the rapid rise and fall of his chest against her back. She lifted a hand to stroke his jaw and relished in his smooth, freshly shaven skin against her cheek and palm.

His thumbs buffeted her nipples until she wanted to moan, but then he drew back and whisked her bra from her shoulders. The air stirred around her. His lips sipped from her nape and then inched down her vertebrae, one soft, wet kiss at a time until he reached her panties. He hooked his fingers in the elastic and drew them down her legs. Andrea stepped out of the fabric and waited, quivering with anticipation for Clay's next move.

He cupped her elbow and led her toward her raised bathtub. "Into the tub."

He didn't release her until she'd sunk chest deep into the warm water. The jets turned on and the bubbling, swirling water teased her aroused skin like a lover's caresses. But she didn't want the jets, she wanted Clay.

"I'll be back in ten minutes. Relax." And then his mouth covered hers. His tongue sliced through her lips and stroked deeply, hungrily. Andrea lifted her wet hands to hold him close, but Clay pulled back. He pressed a wineglass into her hand. "Keep the blindfold on and don't move. I don't want you to get hurt."

And then he left her. She couldn't hear his footsteps over the rush of the whirlpool, but it was as if the energy drained from the room.

He didn't want her to get hurt. What did that mean?

Andrea sat up and lifted one corner of the blindfold. Her bathroom glowed in the flickering light of a dozen candles each in its own silver dish. Clay must have brought them, because they weren't hers. The romantic gesture squeezed her heart. Their lovemaking in the past had been mostly hurried encounters. The few times they'd been able to linger had been in the close confines of his sailboat's tiny cabin. There had never been candles or blindfolds, just raw, rushed passion.

Don't fall for him. He's probably perfected this technique on a dozen other women since dumping you.

Leaning back, she tried to recall the pain, embarrassment and confusion of his abandonment, but it wasn't as easy as before.

She released the blindfold and set her wine aside. Her head was already spinning without more wine. If Clay intended to seduce her then he was doing a fine job, but why make the effort when he had to know from her "pack an overnight bag" instructions that they'd end up in bed without all the extra work?

The air swirled around her shoulders and then the whirlpool jets died. He'd returned. Her pulse raced and her mouth dried. What did he have planned next?

Ten

Clay wanted to be in control, but dammit, he was losing it like some damned high school kid.

All afternoon he'd thought about bathing Andrea, sliding into the big tub with her, pulling her into his lap and lathering every inch of her delectable body with his bare hands, but as soon as he'd undressed her he'd known that wouldn't be possible without coming prematurely, so he'd retreated. Whatever ground he'd gained on his rampant libido by cleaning the kitchen had vanished the minute he reentered the steamy bathroom.

This night was all about Andrea, about showing her how good it could be between them and regaining her trust, but he was about to burst a vein. His gaze narrowed on the eye covering. "You peeked."

She bit her lip. "I—"

"Don't deny it. There's a wet fingerprint on the blindfold." He stroked her cheek beneath the fabric. "Lucky for you I'm a forgiving guy."

Are you? You haven't forgiven your father.

Clay shoved the intrusive thought aside. "Stand."

Andrea rose. Water cascaded over her flushed skin. Droplets quivered on her erect nipples. The ounce of blood circulating in his brain raced south, and his breath whistled through his clenched teeth. Desire pulsed insistently between his legs. He considered throwing the thick bath towel on the floor and taking her right here, but then he recalled the rose petals and the peppermint foot lotion waiting in the bedroom.

Damn. He might not make it through a foot massage.

"How many other women have you spoiled like this?"

Taken aback by her question, Clay paused. He'd had other lovers, but those relationships had always been about sex, the you-do-me-I'll-do-you type. There'd been nothing intimate beyond the physical component. He'd never tried to get to know any of the women on more than a superficial level, but he wanted to get inside of Andrea—inside *her head,* not just her body. Although getting inside her body topped his priority list at the moment—preferably before he shot off like a fire extinguisher.

"None. They weren't worth the effort."

Clay wrapped his hand around her bicep and helped her from the tub and then snatched up the towel and looped it over her back. He couldn't wait. With a swift tug she stumbled against him. Her wet breasts soaked his shirt and her legs spliced with his, dampening his pants. He didn't care.

Her hands slid upward, tangled in his hair and then she yanked him down for a kiss. Clay surrendered. He had no fight left. He opened his mouth, giving her access to devour him. She rose on tiptoe, sliding her pelvis against his. Stars exploded behind his eyelids and a groan rumbled from his chest. He vaguely recalled he was supposed to be drying her, but he made only a halfhearted attempt before he dropped the towel and filled his palms with her warm, damp behind. He loved the feel of her, the shape of her, the taste of her.

He loved her. Period.

Her nails raked down his back. She squeezed his butt and he knew he was a goner. He released her and reached for the buttons of his shirt, but his clumsy fingers weren't up to the task. He swore.

Andrea took over, blindly feeling her way down his chest, opening his shirt and then hooking her fingers behind his belt. Leather slipped free, quickly followed by the hook and zip of his pants. Her palm opened over his stretched boxers and his knees buckled. He sank down on the edge of the tub which put him exactly at breast level.

"Damned fine view," he muttered before opening his mouth over one dusky-tipped breast.

Andrea's fingers tangled in his hair, holding him while he licked, suckled and nipped.

He caressed her waist, her hips, and then his fingers found damp, slick curls. Andrea's nails dug into his scalp and she whimpered. Knowing she was already this hot, this wet for him made waiting almost unbearable, but Clay fought off his need and stroked her.

She shifted her stance, opening for him, and her hips thrust to meet his fingers. Her legs shook visibly. He knew she was close by the flush on her cheeks and her choppy breathing. And then she shuddered in his hand, against his lips and collapsed on him. He caught her, rose and carried her to the bed where he lowered her to the center of the mattress.

She jerked upright, spreading her hands over the sheets. "What is this?"

He pushed her back down with one hand and reached for the condom with the other. The foot massage would have to wait. "Rose petals."

Scooping up a handful, he rained the cool petals down on her skin. Hell, they'd probably leave peach-colored stains on her sheets, but he'd read somewhere that women liked rose petals.

He rolled on the latex, leaned over her to taste the smile on her swollen lips and then hooked her legs over his arms. He found her slick center and thrust home. Her gasp sucked the air from his lungs. When he inhaled, the scent of crushed roses filled his nostrils. He pounded into the tight, slick sleeve of her body. Deeper. Harder. Faster. He ground his hips against hers and when she bowed off the bed, crying out as another climax rocked her, he lost it.

His orgasm knocked the breath from his lungs and made his head spin as if a rogue wave had lifted him and slammed him against the beach. He gasped and groaned and then landed like a washed-up surfer in Andrea's arms. His lungs burned and his muscles disintegrated. He hoped to hell he wasn't crushing her because he couldn't move if his life depended on it.

Her hand smoothed his hair, his face. He lifted a weighted eyelid in time to see her tug off the blindfold. Her satisfied smile melted his heart. "Next time you wear this."

Damn, he loved her. He hadn't thought it possible to love her more than before, but he did. Andrea was a stronger and more confident woman and a kinder and more generous one than the girl he'd left behind. That made loving her even easier than before. And more dangerous.

Leaving her last time had been hard, and he knew with

absolute certainty he wasn't strong enough to leave her again. He'd do whatever it took to keep Andrea in his life—even call a truce with his father.

She wanted him more than before, Andrea admitted with a sinking heart as she lay in bed staring at her ceiling in the early morning light and listening to the sounds of Clay in the adjoining bathroom. And that was scary ground to tread.

It was more than the fabulous sex. Clay listened intently, as if each word carried the weight of a thousand words, not just to her but to each member of the Dean staff—from the high school kid who swept the floors to Peter, the production manager.

The hotheaded high school boy she'd fallen in love with so long ago had become an even-tempered man. Some of the more stubborn employees' unwelcoming attitudes had given Clay plenty of reason to lose his temper, but not once had he lost his cool.

His appeal also lay in the kindness he'd shown to her brother. Surely between Clay's work for Dean and managing his own business long distance he didn't have time to take Tim under his wing. But that hadn't stopped him.

And then there was the way he'd seduced her senses. Yes, she knew what he was up to. By using the blindfold last night he'd put her in the position of having to trust him to feed her, bathe her and pleasure her without going too far or making her uncomfortable. His plan had worked with devastating effectiveness. Why didn't she feel manipulated?

Trust him, he'd said. She wanted to, but how could she when she still didn't know why he'd left her or what she'd done to cause the rift between him and Joseph? What could have been so important that each man would stubbornly stand his ground to the point of forfeiting family? And what would it take to make Clay come clean?

She turned her head and checked the clock. Only a few more minutes before she had to get up and get ready for work. She didn't have time to tie him to the bed and entice the answers out of him. She smiled and wiggled her fingers and toes beneath the sheets. When had she become kinky?

The bathroom door opened and Clay paused on the threshold. "You're awake."

He'd showered, shaved and dressed in charcoal pants and a pale blue shirt. The smell of his cologne drifted to her on a cloud of steam. He looked and smelled edible and she wanted to drag him back to bed, but they had new clients to meet this morning. And she had to get a handle on the soft, mushy feelings inside.

Pull back while you still can.

With a flash of clarity Andrea realized that's exactly what she'd done with every relationship in the past eight years. She'd pulled back. As soon as she started feeling comfortable enough to take the next step she erected barriers or looked for excuses to end it before she got hurt.

She shook off the disturbing discovery and looked up to find Clay studying her. "I'm sorry I didn't get up in time to shower with you."

Passion flared in his eyes. "And then we would have been late for work. We'll make up for it tonight."

She shook her head. "It's Friday. Girls' night out."

His eyes narrowed and his jaw shifted. "Think you could convince my mother to join you if I stay with Dad?"

"Yes. Absolutely." She didn't even stop to think about how she'd accomplish that impossible mission. If it would get Clay and his father together, then maybe they could settle their differences.

"And then I can come here afterward and spend the weekend there—" he nodded at the bed "—with you."

Her mouth dried and her heart jolted into a rapid clip-clop. *You're in too deep. Retreat.* But she couldn't. Not yet. Not until she had her answers. "Sounds promising."

He crossed the room in a few long strides, planted his arms on either side of her, trapping her beneath the sheet, and then he lowered his head and kissed her breathless.

He withdrew and swiped a thumb over her damp lips. "I'll see you at work."

And then he grabbed his duffel bag and left.

Andrea fisted her hands and waited for her pulse to settle. Could she have him in her home all weekend without losing her heart? Other women had affairs that went nowhere all the time. So why couldn't she?

She threw back the covers and rose. This time when Clay left Wilmington there would be no broken hearts, no broken promises and no regrets. Thanks for the memories, she'd tell him, and that's all it would be. Fond memories.

She shook her head and headed for the shower. That was a marketing pitch even she had trouble swallowing. She hoped it didn't come back to bite her.

"Thank you for coming over, dear. I promise I won't be late," Clay's mother said.

"Take your time, Mom." He kissed her cheek and urged her toward the door. "Enjoy girls' night out."

She balked as if suddenly having second thoughts. "But Dora's already gone for the day and—"

"And I have your cell number if I need you. Go. Have fun." Andrea had worked magic on more than just him. She'd called his mother and coerced her into going out.

Heat shot through Clay's veins as he recalled the past

twenty-four hours. Sometime in the middle of the night Andrea had made good on her promise to blindfold him and then she'd driven him absolutely out of his mind. Suffice to say they hadn't had much sleep last night, and he didn't plan to let her catch up tonight or tomorrow night. He shoved his hands in his jeans pockets, adjusting the suddenly snug fit. He had to quit thinking about Andrea unless he wanted to greet his father with a boner.

Clay closed the door behind his mother and waited until her car pulled out of the driveway before joining his father in the living room. He had questions, but surprisingly, the rage he'd felt on his last visit no longer rode his back.

He grabbed the deck of cards off the end table. "Poker?"

Joseph shook his head. "No games. We need to talk about what happened eight years ago."

His father enunciated each word carefully, reminding Clay what Andrea had said about his speech being affected by the stroke. And that's when it hit Clay. He could have lost his father.

Emptiness yawned inside him. He sat down in the wing chair to the right of his father's. As much as he hated hearing about the past, he would have hated losing his father without understanding the dangerous path he'd taken. "Just tell me why."

"No good excuse." His father swallowed hard and looked away. From this side the effects of the stroke weren't visible, and it occurred to Clay that they should have had this conversation eight years ago, but back then Clay had been too hotheaded and too afraid to listen. Afraid of what he'd hear. Afraid he'd find the same selfish bastard lurking inside himself.

"We were having problems, your mother and me.

Business was down, and I was working too many hours and neglecting her. She started sneaking around. Going out three mornings a week, but never mentioned it when I asked her about her day."

Clay's heart pounded like a pile driver. For eight years he'd cursed his father. He'd never considered there might be two sides to the story or that his parents' "perfect" marriage might have been in trouble before his father cheated. Living out of state for five years had kept him out of touch in more ways than just the physical.

"I thought she was having an affair. That she didn't want me anymore. Couldn't blame her. I'd been a testy jackass. Elaine's attention bolstered my dented ego. It went too far. I thought I was getting even, but—" His father's voice broke and his face crumpled. On edge, Clay waited with a knot twisting in his gut for his father to regain his composure. He'd wanted to know the truth and now conversely, he didn't. What would it change? He passed his father a tissue.

Joseph mopped his eyes. "Patricia was taking a stained glass class from that Prescott girl. Andrea's friend. What's her name?"

"Holly." Holly Prescott had been one of Andrea's best friends.

"Yes. Holly. Patricia was making a present. For me. Didn't want to ruin the surprise by telling me where she was going."

Whatever Clay had expected that wasn't it. He'd never condone what his father and Elaine had done, but having heard both sides of the story, he was beginning to understand how two people could make such terrible choices.

He blew out the tension knotting his muscles. "Mom made the seascape hanging in your office window?"

His father nodded. "She wanted to cheer me up."

"It's nice. I'll bring it home. You can hang it here." Clay hesitated, but knew he had to ask. "What about Tim?"

His father's chest rose on a long slow inhalation, and then his jaw shifted and his eyes filled with regret. "He's a fine boy."

"He's your son. You have to see that."

Fresh tears filled his father's eyes. "Wasn't sure. Suspected he might be. Looks a bit like me around the eyes."

"I met him at Andrea's. I thought he was mine."

"No, son, Andrea wouldn't keep that kind of secret."

"He looks like me and he's close to the right age."

His father shook his head. "He only looks a little like you. The eyes. The nose, maybe. The rest is all Elaine. You saw what you wanted to see."

Clay grimaced. Had he been that desperate for a tie to Andrea? Yeah, probably, since he'd just figured out that he still loved her the night before he'd met Tim. "What will you do about him?"

"Nothing. Claiming him would hurt too many people. Harrison is good to him. He loves that boy and Tim worships his daddy. I wouldn't jeopardize that for the world."

"Does Mom know?"

"Don't think so. Hope not. She knows I had an affair, but not when. The affair hurt her enough. Knowing Tim was mine when she couldn't have more babies would hurt even more. She had a rupture when you were born. I almost lost her. A hysterectomy saved her. But it meant no more babies."

"I didn't know."

"Makes her feel less of a woman to be missing parts, so we don't discuss it." Joseph reached across the space between them and covered Clay's fist on the arm of the chair. "I was wrong, Clay. Wrong to cheat. Wrong to ask

you to lie. Wrong to drive you away from your heritage."
His grip tightened. "But you were wrong to hurt Andrea."

"I'm working on making that right. I still love her, Dad.
I want her to come back to Miami with me."

Joseph's hand slid away and his shoulders stooped. "She
deserves to be happy and so do you. Here or in Miami."

"What will happen to Dean when I leave?"

His father stared out the window. "I can't return full-
time. Doctors tap dance around the truth, but I know.
And I want to spend my remaining days with your
mother not tied to a desk. If you're not interested in
taking over, we'll sell. We're strong and financially
stable. We won't lack interested buyers. One of the con-
glomerates has already called. They know I'm down and
want to take advantage."

Clay's stomach sank like an anchor. "A conglomerate
would swallow Dean and close the Wilmington location."

"Probably. But the designs would go on. And the Dean
name would still be on the hull."

Acid churned in Clay's stomach. Could he be responsible for selling out his grandfather's legacy? For putting
a thousand employees out of work?

When he'd returned from Miami he'd wanted the truth
to come out, and he'd wanted the guilty parties punished
for what they'd done. Now he couldn't see that any good
could come from it. His father and Andrea's mother had
made a terrible mistake, but they'd done their best to
remedy a bad situation and to protect the ones they loved.
Exposing the secret would only make the innocents suffer.
Andrea. Clay's mother. Andrea's father. Tim.

Clay rose and walked to the window. If he stayed in
Wilmington, he'd not only have to live with the secret that
had driven him away, he'd never be able to acknowledge

his little brother, and he'd have to continue lying to Andrea. She already had trust issues, and who could blame her? Would he ever regain her trust if he couldn't come clean? But he couldn't. The truth had to stay hidden.

"Clay, I almost lost the best thing in my life because I had my priorities wrong."

Clay turned back to his father. "Mom?"

"My family, son. Your mother *and you*. Don't make the same mistake. You have a second chance. And if Andrea makes you happy, then go after her."

His father pulled the walker around to the front of the chair and struggled to stand. It was painful for Clay to watch. He stepped forward to help, but his father waved him away and then he hobbled one arduous step after the other until he reached Clay's side by the bay window.

"I don't expect you to condone what I did. But I hope one day you can find it in your heart to forgive me."

Clay's eyes stung. He wrapped his arms around his father and held tight. "I do, Dad. I already do."

Midnight. The witching hour.

Sand trickled through Andrea's hourglass of time with Clay. She'd decided before he arrived tonight that this was it. She'd grant herself this weekend, and then she'd do the smart thing and end their relationship before it was too late. Before she fell in love with him again. Before he left her again.

The crescent moon cast a dim light into the shadows enveloping the love seat on her back deck. Wrapped only in Clay's arms and the blanket they'd pulled from the bed, she rested her head against his bare chest, nuzzled her nose in the wiry curls on his pecs and listened to the slowing beat of his heart and the crash of the waves on the beach below.

Thirty minutes ago she'd opened her front door to Clay. He hadn't even said hello before kissing her senseless and making love to her quickly and thoroughly on the rug in her foyer. There had been a desperate edge to his silent loving tonight, one she didn't understand, but wanted to. What's more, she wanted to soothe him, to ease whatever had upset him, and that was dangerous because it went beyond just sex and into the realm of caring.

Pull back.

"What happened with your father tonight, Clay?" She regretted the words the minute they left her mouth. That wasn't pulling back. That was wading into deeper waters. Not wise.

His chest rose and fell beneath her cheek in a deliberate breath. "Nothing. It was a good evening."

Nothing? Nothing had made him go off like a sailor who'd just learned he was about to be deployed on an all-male ship for a year? She pushed upright, clutching the edge of the blanket around her nakedness.

"Nothing?" she asked in disbelief.

"Dad and I talked. After dinner we played cards."

Even in the pale moonlight she could tell he was lying. His poker face and his refusal to meet her gaze gave him away.

Pain pierced her and her lungs locked. Deceit wouldn't hurt so much if she was using him for nothing more than the sex vacation she'd planned. Her fingers tightened around the blanket until her knuckles ached.

She'd gone and done it. Gone too far. Fallen in love with Clayton Dean again.

What kind of fool fell in love with a man who wouldn't be honest with her? Her kind, apparently. Squeezing her eyes shut against the sting of humiliation, she bowed her head.

Clay cupped her jaw and lifted her chin. Andrea gritted her teeth and met his gaze. She struggled against the instantaneous response roused by his fingers caressing the sensitive skin beneath her ear.

"Marry me, Andrea."

Stunned, she opened her mouth, but no sound emerged.

"I love you. I never stopped. I want to spend the rest of my life with you." He meant it. She could see love in his eyes and in his hopeful smile.

Her heart contracted and joy erupted over her skin in a shower of warming sparks. She doused it. She'd heard those words from his lips before, and they'd meant nothing. He'd left her. "How can you say that when you can't even be honest with me?"

His nostrils flared and he sat back, lowering his hand to his lap and fisting his fingers. "Some things are better left unsaid."

"This is not one of those things, Clay. You left me. I don't know why. And if I don't know why then I can never be sure you won't leave again."

"I won't. I swear it."

She stared into his steady eyes and shook her head. "I don't need an oath. I need the truth."

His jaw muscles bunched and he looked away. When he faced her again determination firmed his lips and set his face.

He wasn't going to tell her. She knew it before he opened his mouth. "I need you to trust me on this."

"And if I can't?"

"I'll earn it. I'll earn your trust. No matter how long it takes. Give me a chance to prove I'll never hurt you again."

Her rational side screamed, "No, don't give him the opportunity to hurt you again," but her emotional side, the side that still loved him—yes, *still*—asked, "What can it hurt?"

He pulled her back against his chest and brushed his lips across the top of her head. "Give me a chance, Andrea," he repeated. "I promise I won't let you down."

What did she have to lose? She'd already lost her heart.

Eleven

Everything in Andrea screamed a warning about trusting without truth, but another corner her of mind reminded her that her faultfinding and emotional withdrawal from past relationships had prevented her from finding happiness. Hadn't she vowed to break the cycle?

She leaned against the railing of the porch off her bedroom. Seagulls screeched overhead, begging for breakfast. The beach below was deserted at this early hour except for a few shell combers in the distance. The morning breeze, already heavy with humidity, plastered her robe against her front and promised another scorching hot day.

Clay had gone downstairs to make coffee. Waking up beside him felt good and right, as did making lazy love as the sun rose, slanting its warmth across her bed. She loved him. Everything about him. Except for that damned secret.

What was it her mother said? Trust isn't always blind, but it does offer the benefit of doubt?

Andrea caught her wind-tossed hair and held it off her face. Had she offered the benefit of doubt to Clay? No. Maybe he had a good reason for keeping his secret.

Could she love him wholeheartedly—a marriage should never be based on less—knowing he was withholding something that could hurt her? She didn't have the answer. And even if she did, they still hadn't discussed where they'd live if—and that was a big if—they decided to stay together. She refused to desert Joseph and the company at this critical time.

The glass door slid open behind her and the weight of her decision pressed upon her. Clay, carrying a breakfast tray, padded barefoot onto the porch and set his load on the bistro table tucked into the corner. He'd pulled on his jeans, but nothing else. The broad expanse of his back bore a few scratch marks that she'd made during a particularly uninhibited encounter last night. Her face and belly warmed at the memory.

His gaze caught hers. "Paper's here. You're not going to like it."

Andrea cringed. She'd forgotten all about Octavia's column. She reached for the folded paper on the tray. Clay intercepted, catching her hand and pulling her into his arms. Her heart stuttered and her palms flattened against the heat of his chest. How could she want him again so soon, so badly? And how could she let him walk out of her life?

Big hands cradled her hips, pressing her against a growing denim-covered bulge. And then he kissed her. When Clay kissed and held her she had no reservations. They were perfect together. Totally in sync. She tasted coffee, Clay, passion and the promise of a future in his kiss. Did she have the guts to reach for the brass ring knowing she might be knocked from the horse in the process?

He lifted his head and threaded his fingers through her hair. The tenderness in his eyes brought a lump to her throat. "You love me. Admit it."

Andrea's breath hitched. Confessing her feelings was like reaching the point of no return. Once she uttered those words she'd never be able to take them back.

"Andrea, nobody could worship me like you did last night without loving me."

Guilty. Even without the words she'd given away *her* secret. She briefly closed her eyes before meeting his gaze. "Yes. I love you."

His nostrils flared and a smile curved his very talented mouth. He rewarded her with a quick kiss. "You won't regret it. We'll get married as soon—"

She pressed her fingers over his lips. "Clay, we still have so many things to work out. I don't even want to think about a wedding until Joseph's back on the job."

Clay exhaled, released her and strode to the railing. He braced both hands on the wood. The stiffness of his stance sent trepidation racing through her.

"He's not coming back," he said without turning.

Alarm prickled the hair on her arms. "What?"

"Last night he said he wanted to retire and spend the rest of his time with my mother."

"B-but what about Dean?" Her job and a thousand others?

"He plans to sell. He said a conglomerate has already expressed interest. Although how the call got past my mother I don't know."

The point of no return, indeed, she realized with a heavy heart. Even if she played it safe and let Clay walk out of her life again nothing would be the same. No wonder Clay had been so upset last night.

"You could take over," she offered.

He turned. Reservation clouded his eyes. "I don't know if I'm ready to take that step. But if Dean is sold you'll have nothing to keep you from coming to Miami with me."

"Only my home, my family and my friends." Was she wrong to resist change or was her subconscious holding back, trying to wreck another relationship?

He crossed the boards, took her into his arms and nuzzled her hair. "We don't have to make a decision today. Eat breakfast. Read the paper, and then I have plans for that big tub of yours."

The paper. She'd forgotten the article. Again. How did he make her want to forget everything but him? She squirmed free, reached for the paper and flipped straight to the entertainment section and Octavia's article. She skimmed down until she saw her name.

Rumor has it that the dates have been cancelled, but this reporter has learned that Andrea Montgomery and Clayton Dean can't stay away from each other day or night. Will the former (and perhaps current) lovers sail off into the sunset together? We'll soon know.

Andrea flung down the Saturday newspaper and growled in frustration. "The woman has spies. They must be watching the house because you've been parking your car in the garage."

"Your garage has windows."

Was someone watching even now? Andrea pulled her robe tighter around her and scanned the surrounding beach and homes. "I feel dirty."

"Then let me indulge my fantasy. I have wanted to take a bath with you ever since I saw that tub. You have a decadent streak, Andrea Montgomery, and I want to explore every inch of it and you."

The wicked twinkle in Clay's eyes made her body steam. Because her mind was spinning out of control, she grasped on to the one thing that she knew wouldn't let her down. Making love with Clay was never a disappointment.

Clay brushed off the guilt he felt over using sex to distract Andrea. But he had a tough decision to make and he wasn't ready to make it. Stay at Dean or go? Live with the secret or run again?

Andrea loved him. That was all that mattered. They'd work out the rest. He lifted his hands, captured her face and kissed her hard and deep. She melted against him, soft curves to his hard, aching body. His pulse rate shot off the charts in record time.

"Inside," he groaned against her lips and backed her toward the door. Screw breakfast. He'd rather feast on her. He urged her over the threshold and then shut the door behind them. His gaze burned over her robe. Knowing she wore nothing beneath had him hard as a steel beam. Her nipples tightened, pushing at the fabric, and his mouth watered. He kissed her again, skimming his hands over the silky material, cupping the curve of her bottom and her breasts. When she whimpered into his mouth he nearly lost it.

The tie of her belt resisted his attempts to loosen it. He was on the verge of ripping it from her when the knot came free. He shoved her robe over her shoulders and grunted his approval at finally having her naked. And then he bent to capture her breast in his mouth, rolling the tight tip with his tongue.

She clung to him, but all too soon squirmed impatiently and tugged at his armpits. He rose. Her palms skated over his belly, making his muscles jump and contract involuntarily. She made quick work of the button and zipper of his jeans and then she plowed her hand beneath his boxers and wrapped her fingers around his erection.

His knees almost buckled. Fire ignited in his blood and he sucked a breath through clenched teeth. He shucked his pants and then knelt and found her with his mouth, playing her sweet spot until her fingers knotted in his hair. She yanked until he looked up into her passion-hazed eyes.

"I can't stand when you do that. My legs are shaking and on the verge of collapse."

Clay scooped her into his arms and strode toward the bathroom. He set her on the raised ledge of the tub, turned on the water and then knelt at her feet on the plush bath mat. He pleasured her with lips, tongue and hands until she shattered. And then he realized he was about to explode and he didn't have a condom. Damnation. "Don't move."

He sprinted into the bedroom, retrieved what he needed and then returned to the bathroom to find Andrea already in the tub, a satisfied smile curving her luscious lips. That smile was pure fantasy material since he knew firsthand what kind of havoc those lips could wreak on a man. He donned protection and joined her in the hot water. The slippery glide of her legs tangling with his made him grit his teeth and groan. He dragged her onto his lap and speared himself into her tight, hot sheath. Heaven. A lifetime of this wouldn't be enough. He couldn't wait to get here and never wanted to leave.

Her legs straddled his hips. She lifted until he'd almost slipped free before lowering and taking him deeper. Again and again, she shoved him to the edge of sanity and then backed off, stilling until he wanted to come out of his skin, and then she carried him back to the brink.

"Tease." All he could do was kiss the sassy grin right off her lips and hold on for the ride.

His orgasm hit like a tidal wave, slamming him, drowning him, destroying him. He could barely breathe, barely think. Andrea shuddered in his arms as she came again and then relaxed against him. He held her tight, cradling her head against his shoulder, and tried to catch his breath.

Lucidity seeped slowly back into his conscious. He loved this woman. Not just because of the mind-blowing sex, but because she gave unstintingly. Her time. Her talent. Her love. Her heart. How could he give anything less than one hundred percent? He didn't want to see doubts clouding her eyes. But he'd be damned if he knew how he could tell her the truth without hurting her.

He would find a way. He owed her that much. But not now when his brain was totally fried. Limp as soggy seaweed, Clay closed his eyes and rested his head against the edge of the tub. Andrea slid from his lap and into the crook of his shoulder.

He tightened his arm around her and kissed her damp temple. "The article's right, you know."

She jerked out of his hold, grabbed the plastic pitcher from beside the tub, scooped it full of water and dumped it over Clay's head.

Sputtering, Clay jerked upright. "Hey. What's that for?"

"The article may be right, but I don't want my private business to become company gossip again. If I lose the employees' respect, then how can I—" She paused and then her shoulders bowed. "I guess what the staff thinks doesn't matter anymore. Not if your father's going to sell."

Chewing her bottom lip, she climbed from the tub. His eyes tracked her glistening, wet behind—now there was a view he'd never tire of—to the shower stall. She retrieved her shampoo and then slid back into the water. She filled her palm with the liquid and wedged herself behind him. The coconut scent filled his nostrils as she lathered his hair.

"I want it all, Clay. You and me and Dean. Together the way we once planned."

"That sounds tempting, babe, but—" His words choked off as she poured another pitcher of water over his head. "Warn me before you do that, would you?"

Her hands stilled and then combed through the hair at the back of his head. "You have a birthmark."

"Yeah."

"A red crescent shape," she whispered.

Before he could fathom why a birthmark would put strain in her voice she said, "Tim has this same birthmark."

Oh hell. Clay's stomach sank to rock bottom. So much for finding the right words or the right moment.

Andrea scrambled to make sense of what she saw. Why would Tim and Clay have the same birthmark? Coincidence? No, the nickel-sized mark was too distinctive. The same shape. The same reddish color. And hidden in exactly the same place beneath their hair.

"Andrea—"

She lifted her gaze to Clay's and her heart stopped. Dread, apprehension and she didn't know what else filled his eyes. Her heart thumped with deafening force.

That was the secret. The secret too horrible for her to bear.

"You and my mother? No, that's not possible," she choked out, praying she was wrong. "Is it?"

"Hell, no. I would never—"

"Then how?" The other similarities she'd noted between Clay and Tim paraded through her mind. The eyes. The nose. The mischievous grin. The cocky stance. She'd thought Tim had picked up the gestures from Clay or from Joseph.

Joseph. No.

No.

Her mother and Joseph. Everything in her rebelled at the idea of her mother and her mentor together that way.

Andrea crawled from the tub as fast as her shaking limbs could carry her. Her chest tightened and her throat burned. No. Please no. Cold. So cold. She yanked a towel from the rod and wrapped herself in it.

No.

"Andrea, listen." Clay joined her, but she flinched out of his grasp.

A chasm opened in her chest. "My mother and Joseph."

He exhaled and swiped a hand over his face. "Yes."

Confirmation only made her feel worse. "You knew."

"Ye—"

"When? When did you know?"

He snagged a towel and wound it around his hips. "Eight years ago."

"And you didn't tell me?" She paced into the bedroom, stopped and turned to find Clay had followed. Facts fell into place like a complicated jigsaw puzzle. "That's why you left without saying goodbye."

His jaw shifted. "Yes."

Her heart thumped with deafening force. "What exactly happened that day? You came to Dean and then what?"

He looked like he'd rather be anywhere else. "I walked in on them."

"In the office?" she shrieked.

He nodded. "I freaked out. And I ran."

"In the office," she whispered and collapsed on the edge of the bed. Her mother's comment about Andrea's father being her *first* lover suddenly made sense. "How could I not have known?"

They'd had an affair right under her nose. Betrayal and anger swirled like a noxious cocktail inside her. The ones she'd loved and trusted—her mother, Joseph *and Clay*—had lied to her.

"It was a one-time deal."

She jerked her head up. "How do you know that?"

"I've talked to each of them since I came home."

"And you believe them? Why when they've betrayed so many people? Me. My father. Your mother. How could you believe them or cover for them?"

"I do believe them, but I didn't cover for them, dammit." He knelt in front of her and grabbed her cold hands. She tried to pull away, but Clay held tight, boxing her knees in with his elbows. "That's why I left. Because of the affair. I couldn't stomach—" He sucked in a long, slow breath.

"I came home that day to surprise you. I wanted my father to go with me to buy your engagement ring. It was supposed to be an olive branch because we'd soon be working together. I walked in on them. In a clinch." He spat the last three words as if they were distasteful.

"And then everything I believed in collapsed. Two perfect marriages between high school sweethearts. Both lies. And then I got scared. What if I was a chip off the old block like everybody said?"

Clay released her and rose. He strode toward the sliding glass door. "I got in my car and drove around for hours, trying to figure out where in the hell we went from there. And then the doubts swamped me."

He faced Andrea and the agony on his face made her gulp. "You and I had been together for six years and I loved you. Damn, I loved you. But for five of those years we'd only seen each other during summer vacations and holidays. I was afraid we were making a mistake. Afraid I'd follow in my father's footsteps. Afraid I was setting myself up to hurt you that way."

Honesty at last. If she'd known how devastating it would be she would have stuck with the lies.

"So you left."

"If I'd come back, I would have had to lie. To pretend nothing happened. And I couldn't. Andrea, I couldn't look at them and work with them and forget. And I couldn't stand in a church and promise fidelity knowing that behind me sat two people who'd made a mockery of those vows."

She closed her eyes against the sting and swallowed to ease the burn in her throat. "You should have trusted me enough to tell me, Clay."

When she lifted her eyelids he shook his head. "No. You and your mother were tight. As close as sisters. I envied that bond, and I couldn't destroy your trust in her. My father and I already didn't get along. I considered that relationship no great loss."

"You should have told me," she repeated. "Better that than let me agonize for eight years over why you didn't love me enough."

Clay swore viciously and she flinched. "It wasn't you. Babe, it was never you."

"I know that now. But it's too late."

"It's not too late. We'll start over. Here. Today. We'll—"

"And ignore the bomb under the table?" She held up a hand when he opened his mouth. "Go. Now. Please leave. I need time to think." And then, too torn up to watch him walk out of her life a second time, she turned her back on him.

"Tim."

Andrea gasped at the softly spoken name and nausea rolled in her stomach. She'd thought the situation couldn't get any worse and of course, it did. Murphy's Law.

Clay's hands descended on her shoulders. His touch felt warm against her chilled-to-the-bone skin. But she couldn't lean on him. Her thoughts were too tangled. She had to be strong.

"Think of Tim, Andrea. If this secret breaks his world will be destroyed. Your father loves him. Would he if he knew Tim wasn't his?"

Ohmygod. She hadn't even considered that yet.

"I know you're angry and hurt and you feel betrayed. I've been there, but back then we didn't have Tim to worry about. He's your brother. And mine."

She pressed a hand to her churning stomach. She hadn't even put that part of the puzzle together yet. "That's why you wanted to spend time with him."

He nodded. "I wanted to get to know him. Before you lash out think of the innocents who'll be hurt if this secret gets out."

She twisted out of his grasp and covered her ears. "Stop. Stop it. I can't take anymore. Just go. Please."

Clay captured her wrists and pulled her hands away. He kissed her fisted fingers. "We're not done."

Numbness settled over her. She tugged her hands free and hugged herself. "I don't know how we can go on."

"We'll find a way."

She just shook her head and pressed her forehead against the glass door. She heard the rustle of Clay's clothes as he dressed and then his lips touched her nape.

"I love you, Andrea. I never stopped. And I never will." And then he left her.

Just like eight years ago. Only this time she knew why.

And wished she didn't.

If there had been something wrong with her, she could have fixed it. But this… She couldn't fix this.

The only thing she knew for certain was that she understood and forgave Clay for running because she wanted to do the same thing.

Clay hadn't slept worth a damn since leaving Andrea, which was the only reason he was awake when the boat rocked at 5:00 a.m. Sunday morning signaling somebody had come aboard.

It had to be Andrea. Nobody else would knock on his door at daybreak. He tossed off the tangled sheets, jerked on his discarded jeans and raced up the companionway. He took the stairs two at a time, flipped on an outside light and saw her standing in his cockpit outside the doors.

Relief coursed through him. She'd come. Thank God she'd come. He yanked open the door before she knocked.

She silently stepped inside and dropped the suitcase she carried at her feet. The dark circles beneath her eyes looked like bruises on her pale face, and the way she'd ruthlessly pulled her hair back in an elastic band only accentuated the shell-shocked cast of her features. She looked as rough as he felt. He knew exactly what she was going through. He'd lived this tangle of emotions eight years ago.

"You asked me to go to Miami with you. Well, let's go. Now. Today. Juliana and Holly will pack up my stuff and send it to me. I'll sell the house and—"

"Whoa. Slow down." He caught her shoulders in his hands. He had come to one conclusion last night—one he was absolutely certain about. "We can't go."

She twisted free, paced across the salon and then turned and stared at him as if he'd lost his mind. "What do you mean we can't go? Leaving is all you've talked about since you arrived."

"If we leave Dean, my grandfather's dream dies."

"So? What do you care? It's not your dream anymore."

"It used to be. It could be again."

"Our parents lied, Clay. They cheated. And their deceit cost us eight years. How can you stay here and accept that? How can you ever trust them again?"

"I've been running for eight years and I've finally learned my lesson. Running doesn't change anything. I'm through running. This—" He gestured toward the Dean compound. "This is my life. My future. Our future, Andrea. We have a lot of people counting on us."

She shook her head. "How can you forgive them? How can you forget what they did or live with the possibility of the secret blowing up in your face?"

"They made a mistake. An awful mistake. But they've done their best with a rotten situation."

"You're condoning it." She hurled the words as an accusation.

"Never. But I've talked to your mother and my father and I understand how it happened."

"Well I can't."

"Your mother used to be in love with my father."

She gaped at him. "What?"

"They never told us that part, did they? They went on and on about how we were high school sweethearts just like them, destined to be together forever, but they never mentioned your mother and my father dating. Elaine was in love with him before she lost him to my mother. He was her first love. And you know what she told me? You never forget first love. And she's right, Andrea. I could never forget you, and God knows I tried."

A tear streaked down her cheek. "That doesn't make what they did okay."

"No. Nothing can make it 'okay.' Your mother said that when she hit forty she started wondering if she'd made a mistake in letting Dad go and then things went too far."

Andrea wrapped her arms around her chest. Her entire body trembled. Whether it was from cold or shock he didn't know. Clay led her to the sofa, sat down and pulled her into his lap. He tucked her head beneath his chin.

"I don't understand. Joseph adores your mother. Why would he do such a hurtful thing?"

He caressed her stiff spine. "Remember when you started at Dean? Business was down. That was one of the reasons my father and I always argued. I had a slew of big college boy ideas on how to increase sales, and my dad kept insisting the market would turn back around.

"He was working too much and neglecting my mother. And then she started going out and wouldn't tell him where she'd been. He thought she was cheating on him. In some twisted way he was trying to get even by hooking up with your mother. But Mom wasn't cheating. She was taking a class from Holly. She wanted to cheer Dad up with a present."

Andrea's breath shuddered in and then back out. "The piece in his office window?"

"Yes."

"I remember when she gave him that, but still—"

He lifted her chin until her gaze met his. "Andrea, the affair was wrong. There's no getting around that. But they made a mistake which they haven't repeated and each of them deeply regrets it. And as much as I condemn them for lying, they did so to protect the ones they love. You and me. Your father. My mother. Tim."

Sad acceptance settled on her features. "And that's why

you didn't tell me. You were trying to protect me. From this…this gaping dark hole in my heart."

"Yeah. But my running away wasn't entirely their fault. You have to remember I was afraid I'd end up doing what Dad did."

"Do you still feel that way? Do you think you would?"

"No. I'm not worried about following in my father's footsteps anymore. You've been in my heart for fourteen years, Andrea. You're my soul mate. That's never going to change. I love you, and I always will."

Her breath hitched. "Aren't you worried that I'll be unfaithful like my mother?"

He kissed her temple. "No, babe, I'm not. You may yell at me or dump water on my head, but you'd never deliberately hurt me."

She stroked a hand over his jaw and touched her lips to his. "I always thought you left because you didn't love me enough. But you left because you loved me so much."

Clay's throat closed up. She understood. He closed his eyes and said a silent thank you prayer. "Yeah. Too much to put you through what I was going through. I'm only sorry you're going through it now."

"I love you." Tears rolled down her cheeks. She kissed him again, so tenderly his eyes burned, and then she lifted her head. "Where do we go from here?"

"We have to keep the secret. To protect Tim, your father and my mother. And we stay here to pick up the pieces for them in case the story ever breaks."

Her eyes widened. "That's why you were worried about Octavia digging up dirt."

He nodded. "But I don't think it's likely. They've covered their tracks well." He smoothed her hair. "Do you want to talk to our parents? Hear their side of this? I'll go with you."

She chewed her lip and then shook her head. "No. Not yet. Maybe one day. I need time to come to terms with this, so for now, I'd rather they not know what I've learned."

"You got it. Your secret's safe with me." He smoothed a hand down her spine. "On one condition."

"What's that?"

"Marry me. Build a life with me. And let me spend the rest of my days loving you and earning your trust."

A smile wobbled on her lips. "You already have it, Clay. My trust and my heart. But I have my own condition."

"Name it."

"No secrets between us. Ever."

He'd learned the hard way that deceit could destroy the best things in life. He lifted her knuckles to his lips. "You got it."

"Then, yes, I'll marry you."

"You won't regret it, babe, and that's a promise I intend to keep as long as I'm breathing."

* * * * *

Look for the final TRUST FUND AFFAIRS *book!*
BENDING TO THE BACHELOR'S WILL
by Emilie Rose
coming in August 2006 from Silhouette Desire.

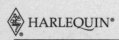

HARLEQUIN®

American ROMANCE®

American Beauties

SORORITY SISTERS, FRIENDS FOR LIFE

Michele Dunaway

THE MARRIAGE CAMPAIGN

Campaign fund-raiser Lisa Meyer has worked
hard to be her own boss and will let nothing—
especially romance—interfere with her success.
To Mark Smith, Lisa is the perfect candidate for
him to spend his life with. But if she lets herself
fall for Mark, will she lose all she's worked for?
Or will she have a future that's more than
she's ever dreamed of?

On sale August 2006

Also watch for:

THE WEDDING SECRET
On sale December 2006

NINE MONTHS NOTICE
On sale April 2007

Available wherever Harlequin books are sold.

www.eHarlequin.com   HARMDAUG

Stability is highly overrated....

Dana Logan's world had always revolved around her children. Now they're all grown up and don't seem to need anything she's able to give them. Struggling to find her new identity, Dana realizes that it's about time for her to get "off her rocker" and begin a new life!

Off Her Rocker

by Jennifer Archer

Available August 2006
TheNextNovel.com

HARLEQUIN
Next

HN53

COMING NEXT MONTH

#1741 MARRIAGE TERMS—Barbara Dunlop
The Elliotts
Seducing his ex-wife was the perfect way to settle the score, until the Elliott millionaire realized *he* was the one being seduced.

#1742 EXPECTING THUNDER'S BABY—
Sheri WhiteFeather
The Trueno Brides
A reckless affair leads to an unplanned pregnancy. But will they take another chance on love?

#1743 THE BOUGHT-AND-PAID-FOR WIFE—
Bronwyn Jameson
Secret Lives of Society Wives
She'd been his father's trophy wife and was now a widow. How could he dare make her his own?

#1744 BENDING TO THE BACHELOR'S WILL—
Emilie Rose
Trust Fund Affairs
She agreed to buy the wealthy tycoon at a charity bachelor auction as a favor, never expecting she'd gain so much in the bargain.

#1745 IAN'S ULTIMATE GAMBLE—Brenda Jackson
He'll stop at nothing to protect his casino, even partaking in a passionate escapade. But who will win this game of seduction?

#1746 BUNKING DOWN WITH THE BOSS—
Charlene Sands
A rich executive pretends to be a cowboy for the summer—and finds himself falling for his beautiful lady boss.